COME ON STEAL THE NOISE

A KILCHESTER SHORT ONE

ADAM MAXWELL

ONE

By the time Zoe arrived at Elsdon Hall the snow had been falling as incessantly as the taxi driver had been wittering. It began when they hit the outskirts of Kilchester and only gotten heavier with each passing mile. By the time they pulled off the winding, country road and on to the long hotel driveway, Zoe had all but tuned him out.

"I said," repeated the driver, "fancy place for someone like you."

"What?" asked Zoe, snapping back into the moment. She grabbed the words from where they hung at the periphery of her short-term memory and replayed them. Her cheeks flushed with anger. "Are you trying to make sure I don't tip you or something?"

"Whoah there, little lady!" The driver was a caricature of a drawing of a white, opinionated, middle-aged idiot. "All I mean was that I picked you up at a bloody industrial estate where, apparently, you live."

"I do live there. And you know nothing about me or

I

my life," she snapped. "Like, for instance, did you know I'm in the habit of recording my life?"

Zoe wafted her mobile phone in the air.

"Yeah, my niece does YouTube too. Are you a vlogger or something? I hear it's good money."

Zoe's brow crumpled into a frown. There wasn't a single thread of conversation this idiot could follow.

"What I'm saying is that I now have a recording of you being a sexist arsehole to me. I could send it to your boss—"

The driver laughed as he pulled the car in front of the ornate colonnades of the hotel's portico.

"Not with the mobile signal here, pet," he snorted and cut the engine.

Zoe glared at him, knowing instinctively that he was right.

"I'm sorry. I don't know the rules for your generation. I was just making conversation."

Zoe looked at the meter and reached into her jacket pocket, taking out her purse. The fare was sixty quid. She took a fist full of twenties.

The driver stared with the same intensity he might have exhibited if she had him by the balls.

She counted out three hundred quid onto the dashboard.

"Thank you—" he began but Zoe cut him short.

She took a twenty back. "Don't assume it's all yours. It's not yet. I mean, don't get me wrong, I'll pay what I owe you, but the rest is hanging in the balance." She gestured to the meter. "You said you don't know the rules for my generation?"

The driver nodded, his eyes darting away from the cash for barely a moment.

"Was it acceptable to treat women *in your day*," Zoe put a particular emphasis on the words, "as animals?"

"I don't understand," he said, his eyes finally meeting her gaze.

"I am not your pet," said Zoe. "It may be acceptable to give familiar names to your significant other. We just met. Not acceptable. I'm guessing if I called you 'dog breath' you'd have thought twice about taking the fare. Also, I'm thinking it wasn't acceptable in your day either."

"Well—"

Zoe took back a couple of twenties. "Wrong answer," she said.

"Sorry," he said sheepishly, but the apology was to the cash that remained, not to her.

"Little lady?" She thought he might have realised what the rules were by now.

"Well, you do look about thirteen…" he said. Then, when Zoe snatched another two notes back he cried out, "No! It's Christmas."

Over the driver's shoulder Zoe could see her sister hovering just inside the expansive doorway. It was time to wrap things up.

"Okay," she said. "Final round. And this time we're playing double or nothing."

He nodded, still staring at the cash.

"If it helps," she added, "imagine I'm your granddaughter."

"Oi," he said. "I'm not *that* old."

Zoe whipped another twenty away.

"You said this place was fancy for 'someone like me'," she said and waved her hand for him to respond.

"Yeah, I was obviously a bit hasty and don't know the first thing about you. Lesson learned." He looked up at her. "Maybe I can help you with your bags and we'll say no more about it then?"

Zoe waited for a moment, letting the question hang.

"Yes," she said eventually. "I think that would be fine. It is Christmas and I may be many things but a bitch is not *usually* one of them."

"Very good of you, ma'am," said the driver and snatched the cash from the dashboard before she could change her mind.

"Don't push it," she said and opened the door.

The cold hit her like a slap in the face, nearly taking her breath away. She panted a cloud of steam, plastered on her best game face and turned with a smile to face her sister.

TWO

Zoe's smile didn't reach her eyes, but she jogged over and gave her sister a hug nonetheless. Agatha had changed her appearance since they'd last been in the same room. Her hair was pulled back into a severe ponytail; the look accentuated by the oversized, square glasses. She usually wore her hair loose and disguised her need for specs with contact lenses. Zoe wondered if her sister was sporting the look because she was straight out of the swimming pool, but thought better of asking her. The last thing she wanted was to start by igniting an argument. She needed to concentrate. To get checked in, set up and ready to do the job. There would be plenty of time to tell Agatha what an utter arse she was later.

"Hey, little sister," said Agatha, exhibiting not one ounce of the restraint Zoe had been stockpiling since they last met.

"It's good to see you," Zoe lied. "Is Gran here yet?"

Agatha shook her head. "I got here about an hour ago. No sign of her."

"The taxi firm called to say she wasn't there when they came to collect her," said Zoe.

The taxi driver deposited Zoe's bags before hurrying back to his car and driving off. Zoe turned to look and, before she could ask, a bell boy whisked the bags away.

"How does he…" she trailed off.

"I've already checked us in," said Agatha.

"Oh, I wanted—" Zoe had a particular plan for the rooms. She'd booked three suites. Two at one end of the hotel and one at the other so she could stay well away from her Gran and Agatha.

"I gave Gran the big suite," Agatha interrupted.

Zoe smiled insincerely. "Excellent," she said. "Just as I planned."

Fucking bitch, her mind screamed. *How are you already messing this up?*

She took a breath and followed the bellboy inside. "Yeah, so presumably she's broken Grandpa Funk out of the garage."

Agatha's eyes flashed with panic for a split second before she remembered the joke and broke into a patronising smile.

"Will you join me for a cuppa?" asked Agatha.

"Remember… Grandpa Funk?" Zoe's smile reached her eyes this time, the memory of them both in the back of Gran's clapped-out old XR3i bleeding through their current animosity.

"I remember," said Agatha, piercing the mood. "Come on, I want to talk."

"And I want to get settled in," Zoe snapped.

"How long are you staying?"

"What do you mean?"

"There is no way you need two massive bags for three days and nights in *this place*," Agatha gestured at *this place* as she deposited the words disdainfully.

"What do you mean 'this place'?" countered Zoe. "I paid for you to come to *this place* so we could *all* relax. I thought it might take the pressure off you trying to make every little, tiny detail of Christmas so *bloody* perfect."

A passing waiter with a tray of glasses paused for a moment by the sisters. "Champagne, ladies?" he asked.

"NO!" they screamed in unison before unanimously realising they were mad at one another, not the waiter, and showering him with overlapping apologies.

They had just calmed enough to realise the right thing to do would be to accept the alcohol and try to relax when someone fired a double-barrelled shotgun at the hotel reception.

THREE

ZOE DROPPED TO THE FLOOR, her sister falling like a domino with her. Glass shattered around them and Agatha shielded Zoe's head with her arm. The smell of wax floor polish filled their nostrils and mixed with an acrid, alcoholic odour.

Agatha could feel damp on her sleeve. "Are you shot? Are you bleeding?" she asked.

"Get *off* me," Zoe barked, squirming from Agatha's protective embrace. "No, I'm not bleeding." Her eyes scanned their surroundings. The windows weren't broken. So either the shooter was inside or—

There was another almighty *BLAM* and the sisters both jumped.

Zoe's focus pulled back and she suddenly saw what had happened. She hopped to her feet, neatly stepped to one side as Agatha tried to pull her back to the perceived safety of the ground. She slapped the waiter on the shoulder in solidarity.

"Gran's here," she said to Agatha.

"What?" demanded Agatha, still reluctant to relinquish to relaxation.

Zoe pointed outside. "We do not have what our American cousins might call an 'active shooter situation'. We have an active grandmother situation. That fucking car of hers is backfiring."

"Mind your language," said Agatha. She carefully moved to a crouch in amongst the shards of broken champagne flutes before drawing herself up to her full height.

Zoe glared at her sister but was forced to plaster on a mask of politeness when a portly man with thinning hair and an immaculate pinstriped suit approached them with palms outstretched in supplication. "My sincerest apologies, Gerry," he addressed the waiter gently but firmly. "Go and get yourself cleaned up. Accidents happen." He waved to an unseen member of staff behind the sisters and gestured for them to attend to the mess.

"I suspect it may be as much our fault as yours," said Agatha, picking an imaginary mote of dust from the sleeve of her jacket. "One of us should have ensured that our grandmother's car was serviced a little more regularly." She smiled benignly.

"Nonsense," said the man. "I'm the manager and it's my responsibility to ensure your stay here exceeds all of your expectations. This... well... it falls below our usual high standards. Come."

For a man of such girth, he was astonishingly quick on his feet and seemed to flick from standing in front of the desk to behind it.

"The… Zimmerman party if I'm not mistaken," he said, his fingers dancing across the keyboard. "I will upgrade you to the finest suites in the—" he stopped dead, his eyes examining the details on the screen before him.

"Is there a problem?" asked Agatha. She shot Zoe a look that simultaneously said 'this is your fault' and 'there better not be police involved'.

"No," said the manager eventually. "I must apologise again. I can't upgrade you."

"I suppose it gets very busy at Christmas," Agatha conceded, trying to extricate herself from the situation.

"Oh no, quite the opposite," he said, eyes still glued to the screen. When he made eye contact once more it was as if Agatha had transformed from a guest he wanted to take care of into the Queen of England. "You're already in our finest suites so, in terms of accommodation at least, there is nowhere further we can upgrade you, ma'am."

Zoe noted he had upgraded his obsequiousness from saccharine to cloying and was using the pronunciation of ma'am usually reserved for actual honest-to-goodness royalty, rhyming it with 'spam'. She was about to interject, to get him to put her back in the room farthest from the family, but he was already too busy showering them with the promise of free meals and wine for the evening.

"What have you two done?" a voice crackled across the expansive reception. Every eye in the place swiveled to see the source of the shout. "Cos you're never too old to get a thick ear, you know?"

Zoe ran over to greet her Gran and it was as if she was twelve years old, running down the hallway to the kitchen, freshly home from school and ravenous for whatever had been baked in her absence. She threw her arms around her Gran and hugged her tightly, breathing in the smell of rosewater and rouge.

"It's been too long, young Zoe," Gran said with a smile. "You better not have been winding your sister up, you little shite," she added.

Zoe's jaw dropped in mock-shock and her hand went to her chest. "The very idea!" she said. "The staff were terrorised by Grandpa Funk so we're getting our meal tonight for free."

"Wine as well?" Gran asked with a wink.

"Naturally," said Zoe. She looked over her shoulder to see what had become of Agatha and by the time she turned back her Gran was heading off at speed towards the bar. Zoe snapped her head left and right between Gran and Agatha before deciding. She jogged over to her sister. "Gran's made a break for the bar."

Agatha looked suddenly panicked.

"Don't worry, I'll meet you there," said Zoe.

Agatha nodded and Zoe sprinted off in hot pursuit.

In the seconds it had taken to bring Agatha up to speed, Gran had somehow gained a chair, a large glass of something distinctly alcoholic and a man in his early thirties. The two of them laughed as if they were old friends as Zoe shambled the rest of the distance between them in utter bewilderment.

"This is the granddaughter I was telling you about,"

said Gran. She put her arm around the man's waist and pretended to whisper in his ear. "And she's single too."

Every fibre of Zoe's being cringed. How had Gran had time to tell him anything? Why on earth was she hell-bent on setting her up with random strangers? Even if they were tall, dark and an acceptable level of handsome. I mean he wasn't her type but—

Her train of thought and any other semblance of conversation came to a grinding halt when she saw her Gran's hand leaving the man's pocket, his wallet between her fingers.

Shit.

This was supposed to be a classy place. She didn't have time for her grandmother's kleptomaniacal tendencies. You couldn't just come to a place like this and steal things willy-nilly. Unless you were a professional thief, of course. Then it was fine. She sighed as she slipped between the two of them.

"I'm sorry for my Gran," said Zoe, not needing to lay on any extra layers of embarrassment.

The man looked sheepish, as if Zoe might believe he had instigated the conversation instead of it being thrust upon him. Zoe turned to her Gran. With her left hand she touched Gran's leg to distract her attention and with her right she deftly plucked the man's wallet from Gran's handbag. All the man could see was the back of her head as she mouthed the words "What the actual fuck?"

Gran's eyes twinkled with mischief.

"Did she fleece you out of the drink, too?" asked Zoe, turning back to the man. "I can't apologise enough."

"Not at all, it's been a brief pleasure," he said.

Zoe had to admit that, close up, he wasn't bad looking, in a generic probably-spends-weekends-watching-football sort of way. Not her type but—

"Pleased to meet you." He held out his hand to shake. Zoe looked at it a little too long before she took it and shook it.

"Ditto," said Zoe. She waited for him to make eye contact then threw the wallet like a frisbee, sending it spinning onto the floor behind him.

"Hope to see you later?" he asked, before draining the last of his glass and making to leave.

Zoe nodded. "Oh," she exclaimed in mock-surprise. "I think you dropped something."

He looked at the ground. "My wallet!" he said, bending down to retrieve it. "Well spotted."

Zoe smiled in silence until he walked out of earshot.

"Nice arse on him, too," said Gran.

"Honestly, can you not behave yourself for ten bloody minutes?"

"Just saying…" said Gran.

"You *just saying* has me scarred for life on so many levels."

"What's happening?" asked Agatha as she sauntered in from reception.

"Nothing," Gran and Zoe chorused.

Agatha raised a disbelieving eyebrow.

"Gran trying to set me up with that tall drink of water over there," Zoe added in an effort not to pique Agatha's suspicion that they were keeping things from her.

Agatha glanced over her shoulder and nodded in approval.

"He's single and here on his own," Gran added.

"Why would anyone come to celebrate Christmas somewhere on their own?" asked Agatha.

Zoe nodded. "He's here on his own? Yeah, that's well weird."

"Don't ask me," Gran drained her glass and slid off the bar stool to the floor. "You can ask him later, if you like. He's joining us for dinner."

Zoe and Agatha stared at her with identical open-mouthed incredulity.

"And dress nice," Gran added. "It would be lovely to have a great-grandchild at some point in the future."

"Wait," said Agatha, reaching into her bag and pressing an electronic keycard into her hand.

Gran kissed her on the cheek and swept out of the bar like a miniature tornado.

"You get mine too?" asked Zoe.

Agatha nodded and handed over Zoe's card. "Can I walk with you?" asked Agatha, a little sheepishly. "I mean we're in adjacent rooms but... can we talk on the way?"

"Sure," said Zoe.

In spite of her request, Agatha remained silent until the lift doors closed in front of them and they were staring at their own blurred reflections in the brushed steel.

"I appreciate you doing this for us," said Agatha, finally.

The two sisters remained side by side, shoulder to

shoulder.

Zoe shrugged slightly. "You always do Christmas. I made some money and—"

"I don't want to know how you earned it," Agatha interrupted. She seemed to catch herself, then turned to face Zoe. "I trust it was... you know... normal."

Zoe didn't say anything. Agatha wasn't the police, but she was one step removed. She worked for an agency called, unoriginally enough, The Agency. As far as Zoe understood it was pretty much a detective agency. Not that Agatha was a Private Detective. It was worse than that. So much worse.

Agatha was what people called a 'white hat' hacker. What that meant in layman's terms was that she had all the knowledge and skills of networks to hack into the computer system of your average clandestine government agency. But instead of doing that or, at the very least, something equally shady but twice as well paid, she chose to squander her talent.

She actually advised the morons on how to plug the holes in their systems. It made Zoe want to reach for the gin.

As if that wasn't bad enough, she used her skills and the skills of her team to assist their private detectives in catching what she affectionately termed 'people like Zoe'.

It wasn't that Zoe was a bad person. Far from it. Her inherent shyness with people she didn't know aside, if you didn't know what she did to make money then you probably wouldn't have picked her out of a line up as a criminal. And it wasn't as if she was a sociopath. She understood that society was built on rules, sometimes even on laws.

Zoe just didn't see why they had to apply to her.

"Was it?" asked Agatha when Zoe failed to respond. "Legitimate?"

Zoe turned her head and stared at her sister.

"Well?" prompted Agatha.

"The fact that you have to ask…"

"But I feel like I do have to ask because—"

"Because of what?" Zoe interrupted, her irritation growing. "Because of all those times I've put on my black and white striped shirt, picked up my bag with 'swag' written on it, walked into a bank and held the manager at gunpoint until he handed over the gold bullion?"

It was Agatha's turn to stare without response.

"No. Because that's never happened." Zoe was working herself up into a fury. "I'm not who you think I am. I'm not Betty Burglar grabbing handfuls of cash from the till at the corner shop or stealing Mrs Miggins' diamond necklace."

"I didn't think—" Agatha tried again, a little more sheepishly this time but Zoe was in no mood for her shit.

Knowing it might be her only chance here in the privacy of the lift, she took a deep breath and let rip.

"Frankly, Ags," she began, relishing the look on her sister's face as she winced at the abbreviation of her name. "You didn't think. Where my money comes from is none of your fucking business. I am a freelancer and I've been saving up my money. One thing I can tell you is that I would never, *ever* put you and Gran in a position where the origin of that money would even mean that you needed to talk to my employer. Legitimate or otherwise."

Agatha looked a little taken aback. She wasn't used to Zoe being so coherent in her counter-argument. "Oh, erm," Agatha replied. "I… well…"

But Zoe wasn't done. "You always do this. You *always* act like you're Mum. Every year you take over Christmas and make everything so bloody perfect without a moment's question about what I might want. You're not my Mum."

"No, I'm not," said Agatha, looking increasingly crestfallen. "Mum and Dad have been dead a long time. But you're all I've got and…"

"I might be all you've got," Zoe could feel the tingling in her lungs as she tried to suppress the emotions. The rage, the injustice… the love. "But I'm not a Barbie doll, pristine and still in her box. I *know* it was hard for you and you shouldn't have been the one who had to be the grown up. We were only… what were you?"

"Seven," said Agatha. "I was seven when I started looking after you and it's a hard habit to break."

"Well," Zoe stared into Agatha's blue eyes. "Well I appreciate it. And I want to help you break the habit." She held her gaze until Agatha finally looked away. "It's not like I could get you a bloody nicotine patch for being a controlling bitch."

The two of them burst out laughing.

"No, I suppose not," said Agatha. "And, it *is* a really nice thought. And I *do* appreciate it. I just worry."

"It's not like when we were kids any more," said Zoe. "You can't just do these things then buy me an iPod and make it all okay."

Agatha seemed to have taken the olive branch. "Oh we played that iPod into the ground."

"First generation," nodded Zoe. "Never more classy than in white."

"And the headphone splitter," Agatha smiled as her eyes stared off into the past.

The doors of the lift slid open to reveal a uniformed bellboy who gave the two oddly intense women a polite nod. They stared at him. He stared back expectantly at them, waiting for them to do something. This wasn't the weirdest thing he'd seen today. It didn't even make it into the top ten.

"This is us," said Zoe. She turned to the bellboy, showing him her keycard and he directed them down the corridor.

They walked in silence until the lift doors closed and when Agatha spoke again it was as if the emotion had been surgically removed from her.

"It's just…" she said. "In my line of work I hear things and… I hope most of them aren't true."

Zoe groaned in frustration. "People see what I let them see. I'm in control. If I'm not then I just jack out."

Agatha grabbed her and gave her a tight hug. It only lasted two or three seconds then she let Zoe go and began smoothing down her blouse. She nodded. "I'll… see you later on then."

Zoe nodded and smiled then the two of them let themselves into their respective suites.

FOUR

ZOE SHUT THE DOOR GENTLY, pressing her palm against it to ensure it was closed, then drew the privacy latch into position.

She was ill-prepared for the sight that greeted her when she turned around.

Grandiose. That was the word that impressed itself upon her cerebellum.

Grandiose and vastly, almost comically, over-the-top. The room wasn't a room as much as a self-contained flat. She suppressed a giggle as the thought occurred to her that the three of them could have shared one suite and still been completely isolated from one another.

Zoe bounded around, sprinting from room to room. She kicked off her shoes and skidded along the floor in her socks. She ran to the bedroom and bounced up and down on a bed so large she had no idea what they would call it. Bigger than queen size. Bigger than king size. Perhaps empress size?

From the marble tiles in the hallway to the gold taps

fashioned into swan necks to the deep, sumptuous velvet of the drapes, the place looked as though Elton John had decorated it. Not late-era married-with-children Elton. This was peak acid-fuelled, laser-queen Elton. It was Las-Vegas-got-nothing-on-me Elton. It was a technicolour, designer-brand money-vomit of excess onto every surface.

And she loved it.

She glanced over at the grandfather clock in the hallway. Just under two hours before she was due to meet Agatha and Gran. If she stopped pissing about, she might be able to pull the job off before they ate.

The bellboy had brought up her bags, and they stood near the entrance to the suite. All of them, including the case containing her clothes and a hatbox containing an actual hat, were padlocked closed. She knew from working with Violet that padlocks were little more than a minor inconvenience to all but the most opportunistic or thick-as-pig-shit of thieves but that wasn't the point. The point was to keep those two classes of people and, perhaps, her sister's prying eyes, away from her stuff.

Zoe grabbed the leather handle on the largest of the cases, a vintage-style steamer trunk that she'd previously adapted to suit her slightly more technological needs. The trunk stood upright and was almost four feet tall and hinged into two halves. The left-hand side originally had five deep drawers and the right side a short rail to hang clothes. She dragged it along the floor until she reached what appeared to be a dining room with a table large enough to seat six people.

She instinctively looked over her shoulder, checking if someone was watching, then caught herself and smiled. It was safe enough here. And it would be even safer once she'd got set up. She removed the padlock then put her thumb on an anachronistic but tiny black panel and the four latches all sprang open.

There was a mechanical whirring noise as the trunk opened itself, the drawers automatically extending to reveal phones, tablets and laptops alongside a plethora of far less identifiable but no less technical paraphernalia. The inside of the trunk glinted with concealed LEDs. Its automated performance was utterly ridiculous and entirely pointless but there were moments where, if you were a hacker, you had to embrace the ridiculousness of that.

The steamer trunk had taken Zoe months to fit out, and this was the first time she had used it, but she was heart-flutteringly, head-over-heels in love with it. Hacking into the computer system of one of the largest companies in the world on your phone while you soak in the bath is fine but sometimes you want to *look* the part. Even if the only person you're looking the part for is yourself.

By the time she had finished setting up, tiny blinking boxes littered the dining room table. Perched next to them were two large flat-screen computer monitors, a keyboard and wires trailing in and out of the steamer trunk. She'd also fitted a series of cameras through the hotel suite for no other reason than she'd bought them a few days ago and wanted to test how well they integrated with her system and what results she'd get in low light.

She glanced at her phone. Half an hour had passed. Not bad. Still enough time.

Enough time to prepare and, more importantly, enough time to grab the complimentary robe and slippers from the bedroom. If you couldn't get excited about the perks of expensive hotels then you may genuinely have to start questioning your life choices, Zoe thought.

She bunched her shoulders up, pushing the pile of the sumptuous hotel robe up and rubbing it against her neck and against her earlobes and sipped at the cappuccino she'd made from the espresso machine in the kitchen. Who knew what else she might find in the suite before the stay was over? She grinned at the thought but for now, it was time to get to work.

According to her employer, the mark went by the name of Quinn Korkus. Korkus was a dealer in the sort of information money couldn't buy.

Or at least the sort of information money couldn't *usually* buy.

It might be an illicit video of a celebrity with an I.Q. barely in double digits transgressing whatever boundary the tabloids currently considered taboo. It might be personal correspondence from high-level politicians incriminating themselves in some international debacle. Whatever it might be, Greggs have yet to invent a pastry product Quinn Korkus didn't have his grubby digits in.

On this particular occasion he had acquired some information that, in the wrong hands, could end the careers of many politicians. Alternatively, it could simply be used to blackmail them to change laws to benefit whoever had the leverage.

And that leverage was every tap, every swipe right, every message and every photo a baker's dozen of them had sent using a particularly salacious dating app called *Kindr*. The startup that ran the app had come and gone almost as quickly as the election promises of the self-same politicians, but before they had shut up shop, the head developer had gone rogue. So, not only was every one of the aforementioned pieces of data at his fingertips, but each and every one was tied to a geographic location, accurate to within around thirty centimetres.

There was no denying who sent them or from where. No ifs. No buts. No coconuts.

And Quinn Korkus was in attendance at the hotel for one purpose — to conduct a blind auction and to sell the incriminating data to the highest bidder. According to Zoe's research, he was due to check in to the hotel today with a view to receiving bids and announcing the winner on New Year's Eve. At which point, presumably, he would come in to a shitload of money and celebrate the calendar incrementing by a single digit. New Year's day would be the day for the handoff and then he would be gone. Into the wind and on to the next job.

Zoe had no intention of waiting until New Year's day or beyond to get her hands on the prize. She'd only booked the rooms until Boxing Day so if it couldn't be done before the day after Christmas then she would face a new set of problems and, if she left it too long, a whole new mark in a whole new location. And that would not be ideal.

Another thing that was not ideal was the fact that she had been completely unable to find a photograph of Quinn Korkus in any of the databases she had at her disposal. And she had a lot. Public. Private. Offline. Hacked. Archived.

And still… nothing.

His name had cropped up, of course, but he had been so careful. No face. No distinguishing features. Despite that, she had to admit she liked him. Or she liked his style. Anyone who could stay that far in the shadows, even from her, was someone whose virtual hand she would very much like to shake. In this mixed metaphor she would also like to slip off his metaphorical watch, drop it in her handbag and leave the building as quickly as was humanly possible.

Except it wasn't his watch, virtual or otherwise, she was looking for. And, she had quickly discovered from her employer, it wasn't a simple case of hacking into his system and stealing the data. Korkus was wily and hadn't just stored the data on an external hard disk or memory card. Not being connected to networked devices would have been a decent defence, after all. Encrypting the data on the storage device would have been an even better defence.

But no, Quinn had style. Quinn had panache. Quinn, apparently, had an inadvertent and pathological desire to impress Zoe, a woman he'd never met and would, if the job went well, continue never to meet.

Quinn Korkus had taken the data he'd acquired and placed it on an analogue cassette.

This fact had thrown Zoe slightly when she'd found out about it. She was only twenty-two years old and audio cassettes had ceased to be a useful medium for music, let alone the dissemination of data, several years before she was born.

This didn't phase Zoe. She was a thoroughbred geek and tech-head and, unlike many of her peers, she had an unparalleled eye for technological archaeology. She had a hankering for the 8-bit era and dreamed of the days when computer games loaded from audio cassettes. Hell, she had an enviable collection of old machines scattered around the warehouse she called home. But those games were microscopic in size. A modern mobile phone could store every game released from the first eight generations of cassette-based computers and still have enough room to store ten high definition movies and a library of music for good measure.

What really intrigued Zoe was how this man had converted the data into sound and how much he'd manage to store on what was, presumably, a pretty normal ninety minute tape. Naturally, this was just the icing on the cake. She'd need to steal the bloody thing before she could allow herself any indulgences.

She took a gulp of coffee and got to work.

FIVE

It took less than five minutes for Zoe to go from no access to having full control of the hotel's network and computer systems. Another two minutes and she had control of their security cameras. Her fingers rattled across the keys, pausing only to yank the mouse back and forth as she took control of the whole damned lot.

The dregs of the coffee were still warm when she began analysing the access logs for room 212. As far as Zoe could tell, he was still in there. The only way to game the system would be to climb out of the window, but he had no good reason to do that, did he?

Zoe had become familiar with Violet's labyrinthine way of thinking so when she checked the hotel register and found there was only one guest in the room she'd remained skeptical to say the least. He could have booked two rooms and used one as a decoy. Or booked his security entourage into the one that was 'his' and hidden himself in the other. Or traded rooms with someone who didn't realise they were trading so that he was in their room and they were in his or…

She shook her head. The dizzying list of what-ifs that Violet would no-doubt have sifted through boiled down to a few basic cross-checks on his credit cards and a phone call.

"Hello, reception," said a voice on Zoe's room phone. She had re-routed the call to appear that it was coming from the hotel's main office.

"Hi, I just got passed this." Zoe tried to sound as bored and irritated as possible. "One of the waiters spilled… I don't know… red wine, maybe, on one of the guests."

"Urgh," said the woman on reception. "I bet it was Carl. He's such a prick."

"Tell me about it," said Zoe. "Manager wants me to comp the room some stuff and my system's on the blink. He's called…" she pretended to check. "Quinn. Quinn Korkus. Is he on his own or with a party or wife or family or whatever?"

"Oh, I checked him in. No, he was on his own. Pretty good-looking, actually. Seen him a couple of times since then and he's definitely flying solo."

"Thanks so much," said Zoe and hung up.

That, combined with the intelligence she had from her employer, felt like it was enough. There wouldn't be a partner or security guard to contend with. Korkus clearly felt like he was safe and in control of the whole situation. She smirked as she brought up the live feed from the security camera positioned just a few metres down the hall from his room while simultaneously plotting the most efficient routes for her access using blueprints of the hotel's layout in another window.

Someone was in control of the whole situation but it damn sure wasn't Quinn Korkus.

She briefly toyed with the idea of simply cutting the heating in his room. The way the snow was piling up outside, the temperature would drop like an anvil from a clifftop, but she didn't feel that was quite the right approach. It would certainly get him out of his room to get warm and, presumably, to complain to reception but unfortunately it might also put him on guard. She wanted him to be lulled into a false sense of security.

Zoe stared at the feed from the hallway. It was just walls, carpet and doors. There was a stillness that gave the impression it might just have been a picture instead of a live feed. She had to be patient. She had to wait patiently. She had to — bollocks to it, she had to piss.

She ran through the suite to the bathroom, made use of the facilities — heated toilet seat, nice touch — and sprinted back, skidding to a halt in the dining area just in time to see a male figure close the door to the room and walk down the corridor away from the camera. Tapping at the keyboard once more, Zoe checked the access logs and confirmed it was him.

There wasn't a moment to lose. She yanked open the bottom drawer of the steamer trunk and pulled out a nondescript black box, plugged it into the computer on the table, then hammered at the keyboard for a minute. When she was happy it was working, she took her spare room keycard and pushed it into a gap on the side of the machine. It ate the card and whirred for a moment before spitting it forcefully back out. It slid along the table and onto the floor. Zoe chased it, grabbing the real room keycard and sprinting to the door. She let herself out and walked a little way down the corridor.

Silence engulfed her as she stood just to the side of a random stranger's room. She waited, listening, in case they were about to come out. When she was sure they weren't, she slid the spare keycard into the lock. The tiny LED by the handle turned green immediately. She was about to waltz inside but stopped herself. This was no time to get caught out by some random guests who weren't even part of the equation.

Side-stepping across the hall, Zoe slid the keycard into the lock on the opposite door and the light immediately turned green. She skipped happily back to her room and opened that too. Back at her computer she checked the logs and found… nothing. Just as she'd planned. She now had a super-administrator keycard that would open every lock in the place and leave no trace on the system.

Perfection. Her last task was to sync her phone with the computer. It was a matter of mere moments, but it meant that she would receive a notification the split second Korkus used his keycard to access anywhere in the hotel. As with even the most basic accommodation, the hotel wasn't inclined to let just anyone wander its corridors and pilfer the contents of their guests' rooms. As a basic security measure, certain areas were out of bounds without the right keycard. The lifts, for example wouldn't move without a quick swipe, the corridors at the top of each flight of stairs demanded you slide your plastic pal through their receptacle and the room positively would not allow you access unless you insinuated your identification into its inner workings.

As a result, she could guarantee remaining undiscovered. As long as she didn't completely spanner the whole thing up.

Walk around like you own the whole damn place. That's what Violet would tell her to do. Zoe drew herself up to occupy every inch of the five feet and four inches she stood in her sneakers and set off as confidently as she could pretend to be down the corridor. At the bottom was a door with two words written on it. When they came into sight, the butterflies that had, until that moment, nestled in the pit of Zoe's stomach suddenly woke up and began flapping like they were auditioning for a role as a hummingbird at the zoo's nativity play.

Staff Only

She reached out her hand and pushed the keycard into the gap in the door handle. The LED flicked green and Zoe pushed down the handle to let herself in. The door swung open. Standing behind it was a man in the hotel's trademarked uniform, with the pinstriped trousers and deep, red velvet jacket.

A deep red that, one and a half seconds later, matched his face.

"WHAT THE HELL ARE YOU DOING IN HERE?" he screamed.

SIX

ZOE STARED AT HIM. The door closed itself behind her and bumped into her back, edging her forward.

Her mouth opened. And then it closed again. She stared at the man's face. She stared at his name badge. She stared back at his face. He was the kitchen manager.

She had nothing. Her mind was blank. Why was she there?

Of course, she knew the *real* reason but she hadn't put any thought into what she might tell someone if she was discovered. Which was a shame, since she couldn't have been more discovered if she was gravity and the man staring at her was named Isaac and was rubbing his head from where he'd just been hit by an apple.

Perhaps she was lost.

Perhaps she was mute, and that's why she wasn't speaking.

"Erm…" she managed eventually, if for no other reason than to check that her vocal cords hadn't permanently powered down.

"Never mind 'erm'," the kitchen manager bellowed. "Uniform. Now. Then downstairs to the kitchen." He shoved her out of the way as he barged past. "Fucking temps in my fucking kitchen, I tell you something——"

But Zoe would never find out what the something was. The door closed itself behind her with a satisfying *clunk*.

Not for the first time in the past couple of minutes she stared straight ahead, this time composing herself.

Act like you own the place, Violet had said. This was what she meant. In this pillock's mind, it was inconceivable for Zoe to be in the Staff Only area unless she was staff. If she behaved in the right way then people would believe whatever the hell they wanted to believe.

She breathed out for what felt like the first time in half an hour then inhaled deeply, glancing over in the direction the manager had vaguely gestured when he was haranguing her. There were a couple of rails where neatly-pressed uniforms hung, each one protected by a clear, plastic bag.

Zoe located one in her size and was soon in the same pinstripe and velvet combo as every other member of the hotel staff. She checked her reflection in the mirror, and was unable to resist the temptation of a selfie before she moved off into the next phase of the plan. She moved at a speed she judged to be fast enough not to allow any guests the opportunity to try to catch her attention but slow enough that it didn't appear she was in a panic.

An efficient power-walk.

As she paced towards her target she once again checked her phone. It appeared Korkus has used his card to gain entry to the gym. This was perfect. She could be in and out before he'd finished whatever cardio-lunacy a man like him indulged in. It wasn't long before she was standing in front of the door marked '212'. She glanced instinctively up to where the camera she'd been surveilling him through was perched, its gaze rendered blind by her interference. She smiled as she pushed the card into the lock.

The mechanism immediately clicked, releasing the lock and allowing her access. For a moment she was surprised when she closed the door behind her. It was a suite not entirely unlike the one she was staying in. Although she supposed he probably made a great deal of money trading in the opprobrious items he acquired.

Like her suite, there was very little in the way of personal effects. In fact, as she conducted a thorough room-by-room search, Zoe began to feel that she might have entirely the wrong suite. So strong was the feeling by the time she reached the master bedroom that she was unable to resist the urge to check her phone to ensure the hotel's system really did list this room as being inhabited by Mr Quinn Korkus. She double checked the access logs, bypassing the notification she had set up to view the raw data on the hotel's server and was *still* certain Korkus was in the gym.

And then she slid back the sliding door of the wardrobe and spotted a large, new suitcase lurking there. On it were two, three-digit combination locks.

She took a deep breath. This had to be it. She'd

searched the rest of the suite. Even checked in the sorts of places people hid things they didn't want found. Inside toilet cisterns — nothing. Taped to the underside of the bed or other furniture — nothing. There was even a cleaner's cupboard which was, ironically, locked shut with an electronic keycard. Even in there — nothing.

Well, nothing but cleaning products and a strange, squat little vacuum cleaner with a disturbingly friendly face. Zoe made a mental note to apply liberal doses of mind bleach to ensure that abomination didn't haunt her dreams for the rest of time.

There was no real reason Quinn Korkus would have been overly troubled with securing the cassette more than by relatively simple means. The way the blind auction was set up was almost double-blind. The customer knew what they were bidding on but not the identity of the person selling it or whether it would be that person who ultimately delivered it. That privileged information was literally the basis of Zoe's tactical advantage at this stage.

Zoe knelt down in the bottom of the wardrobe, the suitcase before her, shelves above her, and pulled at the edge of her phone case. Like a Swiss Army knife, a tool popped out. It looked for all the world like the antenna from an analogue radio, which is exactly what it was. She tapped at the phone and opened an app. It was yet another in a long line of custom builds. Mobile phones were perfectly capable of scanning for wifi signals but old-school radio signals were a different matter. They had the technology but not the hardware. Her addition remedied that and she moved the phone slowly, methodically, around the case, checking for anything that might indicate an alarm trigger.

Nothing.

No incoming signals. No outgoing signals.

She continued scanning, staring suspiciously at the package as she did so.

Still nothing.

She nodded, placing the mobile on the floor to her right, in her line of sight in case any of the myriad systems pinged her a warning. She ran her fingers across the first three tumblers then settled on the first digit. Ever-so gently, she clicked it through from zero to nine and back to zero. She thought she felt it on the nine but went round again to be sure and there it was, just as Violet had showed her, an almost imperceptible lightening of resistance on the nine.

Moving on to the second digit, she repeated the process. Finding the second digit to be nine, she began to think that she might not have mastered this skill quite as well as she'd hoped.

The third digit was... also nine.

Nine. Nine. Nine. She stared at the button that would release the catch. There was no way this guy was stupid enough to leave his suitcase combination as '999' was there?

She took a deep breath and pressed the button. The catch immediately popped up.

Apparently there was every chance he was that stupid. Oh well, that was a bit of a disappointment but actually just made her job easier.

Zoe turned her attention to the other lock. She turned the first number to nine but it didn't feel right. She felt a smile flutter at the corners of her mouth. It wasn't going to be *quite* that easy. She repeated the process as before, clicking through from zero to nine. And again.

It was a six. She was pretty sure.

The second digit... also a six.

She didn't wait any longer and impatiently turned the third digit to six before pressing the button and releasing the catch.

999 and 666. What a prick.

And then her irritation turned to confusion before morphing into a weird sort of respect once more.

Inside the case weren't the clothes of a man ready for a Christmas meal and a dodgy business deal. They were the clothes of a deranged pensioner. Either she'd been completely played, and he knew she was coming even before *she* knew *he* was coming, or these clothes were all part of the camouflage he was using to put any prying eyes off the scent.

Zoe thought about the metaphor she'd just mangled but threw it aside as she threw aside layer after layer of women's underwear, clothes, nightwear. She lifted out what appeared to be a make-up bag and gave it a shake. Inside it, predictably, were the tools in any woman's armoury; mascara, lipstick, foundation, concealer, eye shadow.

And nipple tassels. Red, sequined and heart-shaped and both sporting long, black tassels, Zoe's mind positively boggled at the thought of why he would possibly pack them, let alone the rest of the stuff.

Why did this man have nothing that could be described as masculine? Had he been given the wrong case by the bell boy?

She turned over the nipple tassels in her hand cautiously, as if the tassel might turn into a spider and attack her at any moment. Suddenly the tassels tumbled to the carpet as a voice sprang from behind Zoe like a jumping spider.

"Aren't you a little old to be playing dressing up?"

SEVEN

Z<small>OE JUMPED TO HER FEET</small>, smashing the top of her head into the shelves above. The force sent her crashing back to the floor. She grabbed the top of her head with both hands, the pain excruciating.

A few moments later she felt a hand on her shoulder.

"Zoe, dear," said a familiar voice. "What are you playing at?"

Zoe turned to see her Gran's concerned face leaning down.

"Gran?" Zoe rolled over and sat up, cross-legged, in the wardrobe's bottom. Her head was rapidly improving, but she kept rubbing it with her left hand. "What are you doing here?"

Gran cocked her head to one side and squinted in confusion. "You must have banged you head pretty hard, young lady. This is the room... well, it's more of a flat actually... but it's the one you rented. We're at that nice hotel. I was telling my friend Betty... Betty, I said, I was looking at the hotel on the website and I showed her and she said—"

"Gran."

Gran seemed to snap out of her monologue. "Yes, darling?"

"Are you saying this is your room?"

"Yes."

"And you're not... confused?" asked Zoe.

"Me?" Gran arched a grey eyebrow at her. "I'm not the one dressed as a waitress rifling through her grandmother's unmentionables."

Zoe's cheeks flushed and she extricated herself from the wardrobe.

"You make a good point." Zoe walked past her Gran into the main area of the suite. Gran's handbag was on the dining table and next to it, in a little cardboard pouch with 212 neatly written on it, was her keycard.

"Is this your outfit for the party tonight?" Gran asked.

Zoe's mind was racing, and not from the whack on the head she'd just inflicted on herself. How could this be? She'd checked and double checked. Everything was as it should be. Unless...

"Zoe," said Gran sharply. "I'm talking to you."

Zoe was suddenly ten years old again, about to be told off for stealing sweets from the corner shop.

"Sorry, Granny," she mumbled.

"Never mind sorry," said Gran, a smile growing in her voice that Zoe could feel even with her back to her. "Come here."

Zoe turned around and her Gran wrapped her arms

around her. That smell again. Rose water and rouge. Zoe inhaled it and smiled too.

"Has Agatha played a trick on you?" asked Gran.

Zoe's blood ran cold.

Agatha.

No-one else would have suspected her and certainly no-one else had the computer skill, let alone the sheer audacity, to try to play her at her own game.

"I think she might have," said Zoe into Gran's shoulder.

"That girl can be such a handful, I'm going to—" she began, but Zoe interrupted her.

"No," said Zoe. "It's Christmas. Nearly. No harm done."

"Well that's very big of you, sweetie," said Gran. "Now promise me you won't try to get revenge."

Zoe didn't say anything. Too many revenge scenarios were playing out in her head. The top of the list being the unlikely scenario where she hacked into the computers that controlled the air-conditioning system and sucked the oxygen out of Agatha's room, leaving her dead in the bath. Technically that was impossible, for all manner of reasons, but it was, at that moment, the second item on her list of priorities.

Top of the list was to somehow get the picture of her Gran wearing the nipple tassels out of her head. She hypothesised that mind bleach may be the only solution.

"Promise me," urged Gran, releasing Zoe from the hug.

Zoe hung her head and looked up at Gran petulantly.

"I promise," said Zoe.

"What do you promise?" Gran tapped her foot in irritation.

"I promise I won't try to get revenge on Agatha."

"Okay then," said Gran. "Now you better run back to your flat — erm — room — erm... Suite?"

"Suite," nodded Zoe.

"And put your real costume on for the party tonight."

Zoe tapped her pockets, making sure she had her mobile with her, and began to head towards the door.

"Missy?" Gran asked pointedly.

Zoe turned back, unsure of what Gran was getting at.

Gran pointed at the bedroom door.

"Not before you tidy up the mess you made."

Zoe nodded and got to work.

EIGHT

Zoe stashed the uniform in her luggage on the off-chance she might need it before she checked-out. At this point she had to assume the whole damned job was compromised. She lay on the sofa, channel-surfing in the way she imagined they must have done in the olden days before Netflix. Not that she was watching any of the shows that passed by. It might as well have been white noise. In fact, what she was doing was thinking. Planning. Or trying to.

There was no way she would be able to ditch her family for the whole evening. There was an expectation they would have dinner together and, to add insult to injury, there was a fancy dress ball later.

Perhaps that was the answer. Eat the meal with the family and then blend in with the crowd and pull the job. Back in time for cocktails as if nothing had happened. Yes. That would be perfect.

She would need prep-time, which was limited, given

how she'd been drawn in to ransacking her own grandmother's apartment.

The evidence had been staring her in the face when she'd come back and checked her systems. Zoe was looking for high-level interference and a low-level hack had duped her.

Agatha had pulled the old switcheroo. It might not even have been a hack. If she'd gained access to a staff computer terminal she could have quite easily changed who was in what room. One number changed from a 3 to a 2. Korkus was in the room above Gran. 312.

The doorbell rang.

Zoe picked up a small heavy-duty plastic tablet the hotel had provided and tapped the screen. Agatha's face stared back at her.

Shit.

She could not allow her bloody sister to distract her again. And yet she couldn't let on she knew Agatha was toying with her. Her eyes darted to the computer on the dining table, so incriminatingly set up to make her look like a hacker. She raced over and began to dismantle it, returning its various components to the steamer trunk.

The doorbell rang again.

She'd already left it longer than she should have. It probably looked bad now.

The doorbell rang again. This time it didn't stop ringing.

Zoe pressed the microphone button.

"Hi, Agatha," she said sweetly. "What's up?"

Agatha glared at the peep-hole camera impatiently.

"Let me in, you arsehole," was the succinct response.

Zoe's eyes scanned the room. That was everything. Wasn't it?

Too late now, she thought, closing the trunk and pressing the door-release button at the same time. She bounced back into position on the sofa but the *clack clack* of Agatha's heels failed to reverberate around the entrance hallway. Zoe continued staring nonchalantly at the television but her sister's heels didn't arrive. Neither did her sister nor any other part of her.

"What the hell?" Zoe asked the empty room.

She grabbed her phone and fired a message off.

Where did you go?

Bored of waiting. Came the reply. *I'll meet you downstairs at 17:45. Came over to make sure you didn't need anything for your costume.*

Zoe rolled that last sentence around her head. Why would she do that? Agatha had come over to scope out Zoe's set up. Zoe shook her head in disbelief. The cheek of it.

All good. I'll shout if I've left anything behind. See you at ten to.

Why had she deliberately said she would be five minutes later than Agatha had suggested? Getting under Agatha's skin was just so ingrained she couldn't help herself. And yet, Agatha was seldom any different.

Zoe glanced at the time in the corner of the phone's screen. She had less than an hour and a half.

It was doable. But the plan would have to be watertight.

NINE

ZOE CHECKED the time on her phone as she walked downstairs. It was 5:50 p.m. Perfectly late. Agatha would be waiting but she wouldn't be fretting. Her phone would have been having a fit if Agatha was fretting, bursting at the seams with messages and missed calls. As it was, there was nothing so she slipped it into her jacket pocket before adjusting her hat and fastening the buttons on her waistcoat. Zoe had put a lot of thought and effort into her outfit. It was a Christmas Ball, so she was expecting a surfeit of Santas, plenty of 'sexy' elves, fat men dressed as snowmen and that sort of thing.

She wasn't expecting a great deal of imagination from the guests.

After much consideration, Zoe had opted to dress as Noddy Holder, the lead singer of the glam-rock band Slade. Their song 'Merry Christmas Everybody' was one of the best, in Zoe's opinion, and certainly the most ubiquitous and uplifting of all the Christmas songs. Best of all, being a glam-rock band, the outfit was more than memorable.

And so she had pulled on the bright red shirt and buttoned it up to its oversized collars. She had slipped into the black and white tartan trousers with their matching jacket and waistcoat. She had pulled on the gold, glittery, four inch platform Doc Marten boots with silver toe-caps.

And finally she'd placed on her head the pièce de résistance; a top hat adorned with around forty small, circular mirrors.

Zoe was certain that no-one else in the place would have the same costume as her. And as she threw open the doors and entered the throng she was proved correct in the worst possible way.

Her eyes darted this way and that as heads began to turn and face her. Her cheeks flushed with utter embarrassment as she scanned the crowds.

Not one Santa Claus. Not a snowman to be seen and not one elf, sexy or otherwise.

Everyone was in fancy dress, yes. But no-one wore anything that could even remotely be described as 'Christmassy'. It would be okay, she thought, her gaze caught by a woman on her way to the toilets dressed as Spider-Gwen. She could follow her, somehow knock her unconscious, steal her costume and—

"What the hell have you come as?" Agatha's all-too-familiar voice punctured Zoe's nefarious plan.

"Hey, sis," said Zoe steeling herself. "What do you mean?"

"What's with… all of this?" Agatha asked again, this

time waving a gloved hand from head to toe in Zoe's vicinity.

Noticing that Gran wasn't yet there, Zoe thought about getting into it with her sister over her (thus far, successful) attempts to sabotage her holiday heist, but thought better of it. An argument of that magnitude this early in the evening's proceedings would just upset Gran when she did arrive. Besides, if Agatha thought she had the upper hand, that meant Zoe had the upper hand.

Didn't it?

"What do you mean?" Zoe ventured, confused by her own mental circles, as well as whatever the hell Agatha was getting at.

Agatha stepped directly in front of Zoe, who finally got the full effect of the outfit her older sister was wearing. It looked so expensive it could be exchanged for a three-bedroomed town house in an upmarket part of London, and you'd still have change for a slap-up meal for two at a Michelin-starred restaurant.

"What?" Agatha asked, beginning to panic. She patted herself and examined the little black dress she was sporting before her long, black-gloved hands whipped to her neckline to ensure the show-stopping pearl and diamond necklace was still where she'd left it moments earlier. "What's the matter?"

"Nothing," said Zoe. "Nothing's the matter. You look... beautiful. Glamorous."

Agatha's cheeks flushed with embarrassment.

"Is it the actual one she wore in *Breakfast at*

Tiffany's?" asked Zoe, circling her sister, who shifted awkwardly at the attention.

"No," said Agatha firmly. "I mean, it's vintage Givenchy, but it's not 'as worn by Audrey Hepburn' if that's what you're asking." She caught Zoe's gaze resting on the necklace.

"And that's costume jewellery, so don't get any ideas." Agatha took a step back and smoothed down the dress. It stretched all the way to her ankles and made her legs look ridiculously long.

"What do you mean, 'any ideas'?" Zoe said, Agatha's accusation of her being a thief leaving an unpleasant taste in her mouth. However true it might be. "If you think I'd steal from my sister—"

"Relax," interrupted Agatha. "I'm kidding."

"So why's there no Christmas connection?" asked Zoe.

"Christmas connection?"

"Christmas connection," affirmed Zoe.

Agatha adjusted the tiara that sat where her bun met her head. "I don't follow... ohhhhh, now I see."

Agatha grinned but Zoe could see the sympathy on her face. "Welcome to the Christmas Fancy Dress Ball," said Agatha. "Inasmuch as it is a Fancy Dress Ball at Christmas. On the other side of the invitation—"

"Invitation?" asked Zoe. "Side?"

"Do you ever check your post?"

"Once. At the turn of the century. Who sends anything by post?"

"If you *had* checked your post, you might have

learned that this is a themed ball," said Agatha with
some relish.

"Themed?"

"Themed," confirmed Agatha.

"And what was the theme?" asked Zoe, deflating like
a hot-air balloon suffering an acute shotgun puncture.

"Classic movie stars."

Zoe shook her head, the weight of the heavy hat
shifting awkwardly, then she looked down at her glittery
Doc Martens.

"Never mind," said Agatha, gliding towards her
sister like the spirit of Audrey Hepburn and linking
arms. "No-one will notice. Let's find Gran."

Zoe's brain shifted from flight to fight over her outfit
snafu and the two of them began to circulate in search
of Gran.

"Even assuming it was a Christmas theme," said
Agatha tentatively, "it's a pretty tenuous connection,
isn't it?"

"'Merry Christmas Everybody' is one of the most
popular songs ever recorded," countered Zoe.

Agatha shrugged, her eyes scanning the assembled
throng. "I mean it's no 'All I Want For Christmas Is
You', is it?"

Zoe took a deep breath. "I will concede that, taking
into account the American market, Mariah Carey may
be a little more popular than Slade."

"And, presumably, a much easier outfit to pull
together?"

"Perhaps. But I would sooner slice out my own vocal

cords and feed them to Gran's cat than pay tribute to that… that… crime against music."

"Woah there," said Agatha. "Crime? I mean, I'm not a huge fan, but—"

"If I never have the extreme displeasure to endure that warbling melody-massacre again, it will be a millennia too soon. You know that part when she does the…" Zoe trailed off and began to sing a soaring off-key scale while simultaneously tapping her throat to imitate the staccato runs of the singer. She stopped abruptly as a man dressed as Batman stopped mid-conversation to stare at her.

"Well I like her," said Agatha. "I think you're just embittered by the fact you've come as…"

"As a seventies glam icon," said Zoe, beginning to regain her swagger. "Noddy Holder was one of the greatest frontmen of all time."

"Before my time. Before *our* time, actually."

"And technically he was a movie star cos Slade made a movie."

Agatha rolled her eyes as the pair continued to pick their way through the bustling reception. There was a definite air of bonhomie, the jollity of the season permeating even the stoniest of hearts. As the bearer of a relatively stony heart herself, even Zoe began to feel imbued with goodwill.

To a point.

"Who's Gran come as?" she asked, snatching a glass of wine from a passing waiter.

"She wouldn't tell me," said Agatha with more than a little trepidation. "Said I'd know it when I saw it."

Zoe groaned, a mild worry surfacing that, although Gran was generally quite sensible, perhaps they would witness something that could be deemed 'wildly offensive' in some sections of society. She resisted the urge to drain her glass in one gulp and instead sipped and scanned the room for the septuagenarian screwball.

Time was quickly slipping towards the pre-arranged o'clock. The two sisters approached the bar and Agatha commandeered one of the staff telephones, only to find that Gran wasn't in her room. The weather report was lethal in its simplicity since the surrounding roads were now closed and the snow was coming down with a ferocity bordering on the malevolent. In fact, it had become so heavy that it was piling up against every exit, trapping all but the most motivated of smokers to stay safe inside.

With the confirmation she had to be in the throng it became like a cross between whack-a-mole and hide-and-seek. They decided it would make more sense to stick together, Agatha claiming that this was ostensibly so they didn't lose each other. Zoe thought it might have more to do with the fact that Agatha wasn't prepared for her to make a second attempt at storming the castle and stealing the cassette from Korkus.

They both believed that a woman in her seventies, in fancy dress that was likely more dated than either Zoe's seventies glam-rock outfit or Agatha's sixties glamour-puss, would be supremely easy to find. And yet, with the minutes hurtling past like snowballs thrown by an Olympic shot-putter, the elusive elderly escapologist had slipped her proverbial bonds and, frankly, could have been anywhere.

It worried Zoe and it worried Agatha.

Zoe worried that Gran was off somewhere in the hotel getting back to her light-fingered ways and might, at any moment, be caught by a wandering bell boy and hauled to the security office. She did not, however, want to tell Agatha of her concerns because Agatha knew nothing of Zoe's discovery in her teenage years of her Gran's propensity for pilfering.

Agatha worried that Gran was off somewhere in the hotel getting back to her light-fingered ways and might, at any moment, be caught by a patrolling manager and slapped in cuffs by a passing policeman. She did not, however, want to tell Zoe of her concerns because Zoe knew nothing of Agatha's discovery, in her teenage years, of her Gran's tendency towards taking things that weren't necessarily her own.

So, as it had been for the whole of their lives, both women kept their 'secret' from one another.

And then, in a side room, the Zimmerman patrol spotted an incredibly uncomfortable-looking Indiana Jones. He appeared to be signalling wildly to a Disney Princess, a green-skinned Elphaba, the Wicked Witch of the West, and a lazily under-costumed James Bond in a tuxedo with a bright orange plastic gun. The three chuckled and conspired not to help him as Zoe and Agatha passed.

The aggressor responsible for his desire to be rescued was a woman with a long, red wig on her head and a sequined scarlet dress that was split from the floor to the hip and revealed heels so high they gave Zoe vertigo. The sisters smirked to one another at man-eater Jessica Rabbit preying on a helpless Indiana Jones, but their amusement turned to horror as Ms Rabbit tossed her hair as she laughed at whatever word Indy had managed to squeeze in edgeways.

Ms Rabbit's costume was just like the one in the movie, from the lipstick to the dress's inability to fully contain its occupant's ample bosom. Agatha was appalled to see that the bosom belonged to her own grandmother. Zoe was doubly appalled at the thought there may be matching nipple tassels under there.

"Gran!" Agatha's voice squeaked as she shouted across the room.

Zoe dodged through the crowd of drinkers, powering forward in her glam-boots in a manner that was denied to Agatha in her spindly heels. She linked arms with her Gran, smiling at the terrified action hero in the corner as she attempted to whisk the woman away.

"You are a spoilsport," said Gran as they made their way to the restaurant.

Zoe and Agatha were both steadfastly refusing to engage on the subject.

"Because I'm allowed to have male suitors," said Gran, relishing the discomfort on their faces.

"The fact that you call them 'suitors' indicates you should only be allowed male company under strict supervision," said Agatha.

"Honestly," added Zoe. "It's half not wanting to

think of you in that way and half not wanting to see you shagging them on the table."

Gran cackled in response.

"Anyway, one of us should be happy in that respect," she said.

"What do you mean?" asked Zoe.

"You'll see," was all she would be drawn into saying on the subject.

TEN

A WAITRESS LED them across the restaurant to their table by the window. As they approached the dining area, Zoe noticed that none of the tables were free.

"I took the liberty," Gran continued, "of inviting Quentin from earlier. I think you and he will get on very well, Zoe."

"What?" A look of panic splashed over Zoe's face. "No, you—"

The waitress gestured to a table and, sure enough, there sat Quentin. Being the gentleman he wasn't, he didn't get up to greet them, preferring instead to give them a vague nod and continue to examine the minutiae of the menu.

"Shush," said Gran, waving over the sister's heads. "Here he is. And anyway, didn't you say the meal was free? So it's not like it will cost you anything."

Zoe's mouth moved up and down but words seemed like distant memories.

"Quentin," said Gran, offering her hand to him.

"It's… err—" he began, but Gran waggled her hand so he took it and gave it a peck.

"This is my granddaughter, Agatha," Gran went on. "And this is my other granddaughter Zoe. The one I was telling you about."

"It's a pleasure to meet you again," he said. "My name—"

"Take a seat, dear," said Gran, practically pushing Zoe into the chair. "I'm sorry that she's dressed like that. She's very pretty usually."

"For fuck's sake, Gran," said Zoe petulantly. She tossed her menu onto the table in front of her. "If the waiter comes, I'll have the garlic mushrooms and the chicken kiev. I'm going to freshen up."

When she returned, Zoe was disappointed to find that the amorous Mr Quentin had not done the gentlemanly thing and left the table. Instead, she found him deep in conversation with Agatha, who did that infuriatingly girly thing where she occasionally touched his forearm or played with her hair.

As a rule, Zoe flirted infrequently. As a result she was realistic about how she could turn a pleasant smile into an awkward disaster. She made a mental note to level-up and do exactly as Agatha the next time she was trying to impress.

"Sorry, sweetie," said her Gran conspiratorially. "Not sure if it was the prospect of you doing double garlic duty on your meal or because he has such low standards, but he seems to be wooing your sister instead."

Zoe stifled a laugh. "I also deliberately dressed-to-kill," she said, doffing the mirrored top hat. "Inasmuch as 'kill-any-chance-of-a-man-taking-a-second-glance'."

Her gran smiled and reached over, touching her cheek. "You'll find someone," she said. "Either that or I'll drug you, ship you to a desert island and forge your signature so you wake up Mrs Thingummysmith."

Zoe rolled her eyes. "Life's about more than men, Gran."

"Not if you're my age and want great-grandkids, it's not. Anyway, if it's any consolation, I think I misjudged him. From the approach he's trying with Agatha I fear he may be what my girls and I used to call, 'an utter twat'."

Zoe, who had been politely sipping at her white wine spritzer, did a spit take and showered the table. Amongst the apologies and dabbing of napkins, a waiter arrived and attempted to take their order. Once successful, he evaporated, and the evening descended into the usual blur of wine, laughter and glares that usually punctuated a family meal for the Zimmermans.

The presence of this Quentin chap seemed to have put a lid on any major spats. It wasn't just the girls behaving themselves. Gran was, if not behaving herself, at least moderating her usual levels of crazy to socially acceptable levels.

By the time they were ordering dessert, Zoe was having a good time despite the interloper, and had successfully avoided consuming any more alcoholic beverages without drawing any suspicion from Agatha. This was particularly important, as she was famously hopeless at holding her booze and had to be firing on all cylinders if she was to pull off her new plan.

And the best-laid plans of a half-cut thief oft go awry, Zoe told herself.

She stared at the window as the waitress cleared the finished dishes away. The snow had blown into a drift against the glass some six feet tall and she could watch the reflections of the staff and diners without the embarrassment of them noticing she was staring at them.

Agatha and Quentin got to their feet, and she cringed as he patted Agatha on the arse. She was about to say something but thought better of it. She could get drunk and shout at him later, once she'd done the job. Plus, he'd keep Agatha occupied in the meantime.

The ballroom reminded Zoe somewhat of the ballroom in the Overlook Hotel from 'The Shining'. Its grandeur was capped off with an ornate, windowed dome which presumably would have allowed a fine view of the stars on any day it wasn't thick with snow.

She took a breath. It was time. She'd planned to 'bump' into a waiter and get covered in something as an excuse to leave but as they entered the ballroom, Gran peeled off to the bar and Agatha gave her a smile and led Quentin off to a table for two at the other side of the dance floor.

Okay then, this was it. Time to get this show on the road.

ELEVEN

ZOE WHIPPED off the mirrored top hat and pulled open a secret panel within. It came away to reveal a tiny, drawstring bag. She extracted it and reached inside, pulling out a second mobile phone and the access-all-areas keycard she'd created earlier in the day.

Slipping out of sight of the main throng, Zoe skipped quickly down the twisting corridors that led to the main reception. She swiped the key card to access the lift and thumbed the call button impatiently. With a self-satisfied sigh the doors slid open and she stepped inside.

She entered a horrendously long pass code into the new phone and the screen came to life. Tapping at it for a few moments, she confirmed the script she'd written earlier had executed perfectly.

She looked up at the lift's security camera and smiled as the red LED which indicated its active status drained into darkness. Every single security camera in the hotel was out of commission.

Perfect. She swiped to another app and her smile widened, seeing that Korkus had left room 312 at 6:17 p.m. She had what she believed amounted to an open goal.

Still, best not to rest on whatever laurels she had at her disposal. Tapping her platformed foot, Zoe stared at her appearance in the mirrored walls of the lift. The mirrors on the top hat shone like a portable glitter ball.

Second time lucky, she thought as the doors opened. A few paces from the lift was a fire door which, once again, required the keycard. She swiped it confidently, waiting for the familiar *chunk* as the magnetic lock released.

Nothing.

She swiped again.

Again, nothing.

She pulled her phone out and began furiously tapping. Her keycard was still fine. She hadn't accidentally disabled the locks. It didn't *look* like Agatha had done anything, but—

"Are you okay there?"

The unexpected voice snapped Zoe from her concentration. Adrenaline washed into her system but she resisted the urge to panic. Her eyes rested on an elderly couple dressed as a world weary Wonder Woman and paunchy Adam West-era Batman.

"Look, Donna," said the man with a smile. "Noddy Holder."

He gestured at Zoe's costume and she nodded in recognition, as well as at the relief of not being caught.

"I'm a fan," said Zoe.

"Did you know that it was Freddie Mercury off of Queen what sold him that hat?" asked the old man.

"Err, no," said Zoe.

"True fact," he nodded to confirm.

"He does the pub quiz at the Old Ship — the pub in our village," said the woman, rolling her eyes. "Imagine having to live with this."

"Young Freddie Mercury ran a market stall in Kensington," the bloke continued. "He sold the hat to Noddy, and he says to him, 'One day I'm going to be a big pop star like you'. And do you know what Noddy said to him?"

Zoe shook her head, loving this mad old fella's patter.

"He said, 'Fuck off, Freddie'!" The geezer burst into a fit of wheezing laughter.

"Are you done?" his wife asked.

It was Batman's turn to roll his eyes but he nodded submissively.

"Did you not get the message?" the woman asked Zoe. "All the locks have gone wrong on this corridor." She pushed at the door, illustrating her point to Zoe.

"On the rooms, too?" asked Zoe. Was this a side-effect of something she'd done or was it the work of her meddling sister?

"Yes," said the man, walking through the door. "But don't worry, there's a security guard. He's not letting anyone into any of the rooms unless their signature matches the one on file."

"Oh, that's good news," said Zoe, stating the exact

opposite of her actual opinion. "Wait, is this the *third* floor?"

The woman nodded.

"Ah, my room is on the second floor!" she said, putting her palm to her brow. "Silly me. Merry Christmas!"

Zoe turned and walked away just as she spotted the burly security guard over the shoulder of Wonder Woman.

This was absolutely Agatha's doing. Disabling the electronics was… diabolical. It literally took away Zoe's super-power.

She heard the sound of the door closing echo down the corridor but to her dismay it was not followed by the silence she expected. It was followed by the sound of footsteps. She took a deep breath and headed around a corner then jogged along until she reached another and turned again. She slowed down, stepping as softly as she could without breaking pace, but there was an unmistakable sound of someone following her.

Chancing a look over her shoulder, Zoe made sure there was no-one immediately behind her then pushed the handle of the first 'Staff Only' door she found. It was locked. And that was *fantastic*. It meant that Agatha's ruse had not extended any further than Korkus' corridor. Zoe slapped her keycard into the slot and swiped.

The lock opened and she threw open the door. Instead of the maid's trolley and shelves of supplies she'd expected, there a thin, metal walkway and a vertiginous drop fifteen metres straight down to the floor below. Her common sense immediately rebelled, telling her that now was the perfect moment to step back into the corridor and fuck this shit once and for all.

But Zoe did not step back into the corridor. The footsteps were growing closer. Her eyes flicked to the end of the corridor and she swallowed hard before stepping through the door and closing it as softly as she could behind her.

The heat and noise of the room below hit her like a pillow full of custard. For a moment Zoe felt a little light-headed and put her palm against the wall to steady herself. She looked down at the room below and immediately knew exactly where she was.

This was the ballroom. And that was the party she'd just left. She stood on a circular walkway which ran all the way around the edge of the windowed dome above her. The walkway was around thirty centimetres wide, just enough for her to stand with her feet together and have a tiny bit of space either side. Fifteen metres below her was the dance floor.

Not that Zoe saw the drop as fifteen metres, nor even fifty feet. To Zoe the drop looked significantly more than these paltry comparisons. To her it looked like it was the height of three or four double decker buses balanced precariously on top of one another.

She edged along the platform away from the door. She didn't like heights. But she liked being caught even less. The idea of falling had begun to seriously take root and Zoe knew she would need to distract herself to prevent the sort of mental maelstrom that might see her taking a swan-dive down to ground level. Surveying her surroundings, she decided that this particular view only existed for one reason and that was to clean the windows. As such, there should be something to prevent her from falling. She ran her splayed hand behind her against the wall and moments later found a rail.

If she had a harness, it would clip on to that. But Zoe did not have a harness, because who in their right mind would be up here voluntarily? So she settled for crouching slightly and gripping the rail tightly with both hands.

She took a breath. She had this. She didn't need Violet or the others; she was a strong, capable young woman getting ready to steal from a strong, capable man. Chancing a look down, she quickly picked out Gran at the bar with several, presumably empty, shot glasses lined up in front of her. Agatha and the handsyman sat at a booth on the opposite side of the dance floor, getting more than friendly with one another.

She averted her eyes in irritation. Agatha's taste in men was usually so much better than this. There were so many other men here tonight that were much more attractive like...

Well, that man with the ginger hair was... pretty old, actually.

And the Asian guy strutting about on the dance floor dressed as John Travolta from Saturday Night Fever was... not going to impress anyone.

But the young, black guy at the bar. That was a man she could get her teeth into. Tall, handsome and with mannerisms that suggested either he was casing the place or — more likely — he was someone who paid attention. Even his outfit — dressing gown, slippers, towel and satchel. If the dressing gown wasn't screen accurate for the television adaptation of the *Hitchhiker's Guide to the Galaxy*, then she would be very surprised.

As she stared, he seemed to feel her gaze upon him and shifted his head to look upwards. Zoe got a fright and pushed back to remain unseen, but there was nowhere to push back to. There was no way he could see her up here, surely. The sweeping glare from the lighting rig would blind anyone looking up here. Even dressed as Noddy Holder, no-one would be able to see her.

And then, as if reading her mind, all the lights came on and the flashing disco lights were dimmed. The whole ballroom was bathed in migraine-inducing white light. Everyone *must* be able to see her. All she could think was 'I wish this was Violet and not me' as she closed her eyes tightly and waited for someone to shout or an alarm to go off or something.

The PA crackled into life and a cheesy DJ's voice boomed out, echoing all the louder in the dome around Zoe.

"Do we have a Pat - no… sorry… Zack Roach in the house tonight?"

Zoe opened her eyes a crack but stayed frozen on the walkway as the handsome, inquisitive man in the dressing gown was whisked forward by his family.

She breathed out.

Perhaps she would wish him a happy birthday later on. Touch his arm. Play with her hair.

Perhaps not.

With the crowd below distracted, Zoe edged along the walkway to a second door, this one partially concealed and roughly three-quarters the size of a normal door. Finding it unlocked, she threw it open to the tune of 'Happy Birthday', stepped through and closed it gently behind her.

The other side of the door was pitch black but Zoe listened in the darkness for a moment to ensure there was no-one nearby. When she was happy she was alone, she turned on her phone's torch to reveal a store cupboard filled with metal shelves stacked high with cleaning materials.

The place looked like a bomb had gone off, the clutter reaching such precarious heights that the upper shelves threatened to spew projectiles if you dared to glance in their direction. The floor was cluttered with buckets and plastic containers filled with who-knew-what and blocking the exit back into the hotel hallways was a maid's trolley.

Again, Zoe took off her mirrored top hat. Like an amateur magician who'd only mastered one trick, she reached into the hidden compartment and pulled out the only other thing she'd stashed in there. The maid's uniform she'd purloined earlier.

Zoe took off her fancy dress, removing a pair of black ballet pumps from the coat pockets as she did. Shivering, she put on the maid's uniform, before ramming as much of her Noddy Holder outfit into the hat as she could. The rest she stashed behind an avalanche of toilet rolls.

Somewhat satisfied, she straightened her uniform,

ran her fingers through her hair, then pushed the handle of the door open. With a heave, she dragged the maid's cart into the corridor. Agatha thought she'd put paid to another attempt but Zoe knew better. She was twice the hacker her older sister was and she was three times the master-of-disguise. Or should that be mistress-of-disguise?

Zoe pondered the phrase as she pushed the cart towards Korkus' room. It just didn't sound right in her mind's mouth as she said it. Smash the patriarchy and all that, but not at the expense of proper grammar. Having said that, 'mistress-of-disguise' had a certain ring to it. She made a mental note to try it out in conversation in front of Violet, a true mistress-of-disguise if ever she knew one.

"You can't go in," said the security guard when she finally reached Korkus' room.

Zoe ignored him, taking the keycard from her trolley and reaching for the door.

"This whole floor needs doing before the end of my shift," said Zoe.

The security guard grabbed her wrist gently but firmly. "Not this one," he said. Releasing his grip on her, he pointed to the door handle.

A paper sign hung bearing a simple message: DO NOT DISTURB.

Zoe opened her mouth to argue but the security guard began to drag her trolley down the hallway. She kept pace with him until he let go of the trolley but in the intervening time her brain had made a series of calculations, the culmination of which was the decision to use her newly-discovered flirting skills to convince this member of the opposite sex to do as she wished.

She waited for him to look back up at her and then raised her index finger and reached for a strand of hair to twirl. Zoe's dark brown hair was cut into a short bob which, she calculated, gave her just enough to pull off the effect. She widened her eyes in the way she imagined a cat might plead for cream and twirled her finger.

Her hair, having been cut only the day before, was in great condition. Lustrous and silky, it slipped straight from her grip and left her twirling her finger as if she had been implying the security guard was crazy while his back was turned.

He opened his mouth to question her but stopped before the words formed.

In a last ditch attempt at seduction, Zoe reached out to touch his forearm and knocked the clipboard he was holding to the floor.

The security guard's face hardened into a grimace and he knelt down to retrieve the clipboard. "You can start next door," he said, gesturing to the door.

"Yeah," said Zoe, dying a little inside and averting her gaze back to the trolley. "These suites take some cleaning," she offered, desperately trying to change the subject. "Some of these people are like animals."

On the introduction of a more familiar conversational tack, the security guard appeared to relax once more. "You're not wrong," he pushed the door of the next room open. "There you go."

"Thanks again," she said, pushing the cleaning

trolley through. As the door closed behind her the smile dropped from her face.

Bloody Agatha!

It could only be her who'd hung the fucking 'do not disturb' sign on the door. Who else would put one of those up at this time of night?

Feeling like she was losing her shit, Zoe took a deep breath to calm herself. It smelled of shoe polish and irritation.

What was she going to do?

Snapping out of her little pity-party, she surveyed the suite. It wasn't as nice as hers and that made her feel a little better. It still had a kitchen area though. And that meant that it had knives. She remembered Violet telling her about the nightclub job after she'd recovered from the smoke inhalation — they'd smashed through the walls to get where they wanted to be.

That might just work. When she was searching through her Gran's bag, in the bottom of the wardrobe the wall had seemed...

What? What had the wall seemed? She was letting her imagination get the better of her.

What did she *actually* know?

She knew the hotel was originally a stately home, which meant that almost every internal wall dividing the rooms would just be plasterboard partitions.

She knew she could lay her hands on a knife from the kitchen in the suite. She had no idea how long it would take to cut through the wall without expert equipment. If his suite was anything like hers then the cutlery would have struggled to cut pre-sliced bread.

Besides that, she knew that if she left a bloody great hole in Korkus' wall then he would inevitably suspect that someone had robbed him. And if he found out while they were snowed in, things might very well escalate to levels only previously seen in *The Shining*.

So that was a 'no'.

Suddenly aware of how much time she was wasting, Zoe took out her phone to check on the location of the main players in the game. Korkus had not used the lift or stairs, so he couldn't be in his room. And there was nothing to suggest Agatha had moved from the ballroom.

Satisfied that she still had a window of opportunity, Zoe looked up from her phone. Wait a minute... Window! Of course!

Zoe crossed the room to a pair of glass doors. Beyond which was a balcony.

She tugged at the handle but it didn't budge. Apparently, Agatha wasn't as good as she thought she was. Zoe swiped her keycard in a receptacle to the side of the door and the lock released, allowing her to open it. The second she stepped outside, the snow soaked through her thin, canvas ballet pumps. She could feel the chill creeping from the pads of her feet upwards. Unperturbed, she flicked on her phone's torch and surveyed the scene.

To her delight she found that this balcony and Korkus' were adjoining, separated only by a waist-height metal railing. Turning back to the door she saw there was a card swipe on the outside too. This was going to be easy. All she had to do was climb over, let herself in, climb back and she was home free.

The balcony was around twelve feet long and jutted out nearly five feet. She stepped towards the edge to look over and her foot slid on the ice under the thick layer of snow. Catching herself just in time, she grabbed the railing. The last thing she wanted was to be caught unconscious in a maid's uniform in someone else's room. She imagined Violet in the same situation, just jumping over the edge like some sort of action movie star. She peered over and shivered. Looking down into the darkness she couldn't see anything.

Maybe that was better. It was a long way down.

Zoe took a minute, adjusting her clothes, pulling railings, shifting snow, trying to make sure there was as little margin for error — for falling — as possible. When she was satisfied, she lifted herself up onto the railing. In spite of her preparations she stifled a gasp as the snow seeped straight through and froze her bum. That was… not something she was keen on. She swung first one leg, then the other over then slid down the short distance, landing knee-deep in snow but safe on Korkus' side of the balcony.

The curtains weren't drawn and there was only one light emanating from a room she couldn't see into from her current vantage point. To be sure, she pulled out her mobile and checked for Korkus' location. The phone told her nothing except that she had no signal for the hotel's wifi. She made a few adjustments. There was no mobile signal either.

"What sort of person comes to a hotel with no wifi

or phone signal?" Zoe asked the falling snow. She tapped at her phone again. The last time the phone had signal was five and a half minutes ago, when Korkus had still been downstairs in the hotel.

What would she do?

Assume he's not there. Be more cautious. She might get a mobile signal if she was closer to the room.

This was it then. She stared into the room and reached her hand out to swipe the keycard and open the door. The second she swiped the card, a tiny LED turned green and she heard the mechanism unlock. The warm feeling of impending success began to rise inside her and she stood for a moment, watching her breath fogging the glass of the door. But the happiness didn't have time to pull her mouth into a smile before every light in the flat burst into incriminating, floodlit, life.

Zoe's chin dropped, agog, as panic gripped her.

He was there.

He was there and she was caught and...

She spun around and slipped on the ice, dropping to the floor and landing heavily on her tailbone. She howled in pain and curled into the foetal position in the snow. For a moment there was nothing but the searing pain and then, slowly, her body began to reboot. She felt the icy cold from the snow seeping into her clothes and freezing her skin. She felt herself shaking with the cold and, as she opened her eyes, she felt utter fury.

On the sofa was Quentin. Quentin from the meal. Quentin the twat.

Straddling Quentin in a decidedly un-Audreylike way was Agatha.

For a split second Zoe wondered if Agatha had sent her to the wrong room again but — no — not this time. This wasn't Quentin. Her cloth-eared Gran had got it wrong. This was Quinn. And Agatha was, at that second, taste-testing his tonsils.

She had to get off the balcony. Now. And she had to do it without being seen. Edging along on her side, digging through the snow, every fibre of her clothing was soaked with half-melted icy water. She was shaking with what she assumed was the early stages of hypothermia but she was not beaten.

She lifted herself up onto the railing and threw one leg, then the other over. Panicked and exposed she dropped over the railing but the balcony of the room next door did not catch her. In the confusion and the cold Zoe had hurled herself over the edge of the balcony and into the pitch-black abyss that was three storeys high.

Time slowed and Zoe felt something in her stomach akin to what she might feel if she was unexpectantly fired from a cannon as she dropped straight to the ground.

TWELVE

WHEN SHE OPENED HER EYES, Zoe was pleasantly surprised to find out she was still alive. Unfortunately, the pleasure of not being dead was short-lived.

She tried to shift her body, to move and stand, but she couldn't. Her legs wouldn't move. Her hips wouldn't move and, as if it was some sort of conspiracy, her upper body wouldn't move either.

Blinking into the darkness, she could make out some vague shapes. Her eyes quickly became accustomed to the low light and she tried to ascertain the problem. Ever the slave to logic, her eyes looked this way and that to try to establish what was going on. In front of her was snow. The same to the left and right. But she had no body.

Not in the way the singer of a sad song might have nobody. She had no body. No feet. No legs. Everything from the neck down was gone.

For a moment she wondered if it was like the stories you heard about chopping off a chicken's head and the body running around afterwards. She couldn't see her body running about. And she'd been trying to work out what was going on for too long for it to be her head existing independently of her body. There had to be another explanation.

There was a loud digital *chirrup* and, not for the first time that day, Zoe jumped in fright. As she did, the mini-avalanche she was under shifted, allowing her the wriggle room to free her upper body and then, with the aid of some digging, her legs and feet.

She finally stood up, her body practically convulsing from the cold but her retrieved mobile phone clasped tightly in her right hand. She assessed the situation.

What had happened in the air she didn't know, but she had fallen into a snowdrift which had caused the surrounding snow to slide on top of her. She stared for a second but the sound of panicked voices broke her concentration. Her head darted left and right, looking for cover, but there was none. A torch flicked around her and stopped, pointing at her face.

Zoe just stood, hugging herself, shaking uncontrollably and waiting for her inevitable fate.

"There she is," said a voice she recognised.

Hands brought blankets, faces looked sympathetic and a story unfolded of Gran being worried about her. Zoe listened, as surprised as the staff to find out that she hadn't been dangling precariously from a rope three floors in the air but had, in fact, gone out for a cigarette and a walk.

"And when she didn't come back I knew something

was wrong," said her Gran. "We need to get her back to her room and into a hot bath…"

Zoe gave up. She accepted the blankets. She embraced the attention. An hour later she even accepted it when her Gran tucked her into bed and kissed her forehead.

"There's always tomorrow," she could have sworn she heard the old woman say. But it had been a long day and she was millimetres from sleep. She relaxed for a second and then—

THIRTEEN

IT WAS morning when she woke. The night had felt long and been full of dreams of apparitions from the shadows brandishing blunt weapons and the constant sense of falling.

When she finally did switch on the bedside light at just after eight a.m., she ordered breakfast to be delivered to her room so that she didn't have to face either member of her family. She began to search around the bed for any of her mobile phones and, the more awake she became, the more questions began to swirl around her head.

How had Gran known she was outside? Why did she make excuses for Zoe? What was Agatha doing with Quinn Korkus? Did her sister know anything about what had happened last night? Had Gran told her? How could she get the cassette now? Why did she think she was cut out for field work? Why hadn't she asked one of the team for an assist? And what would happen to her if she didn't get the cassette?

One of those questions she could answer and several more were about to answer themselves in quick succession.

She had to stray as far as the lounge to find where Gran had thoughtfully plugged in her phone to charge. Once she was safely ensconced back in the enormous empress-bed, she opened the first message:

I ASSUME YOU HAVE THE PRIZE? I DON'T NEED TO REMIND YOU OF THE CONSEQUENCES IF YOU FAIL.

And thirty seconds later there was a second message. This one was a picture of a clawhammer lying on a desk. The desk was spattered with the same blood that was caked onto the grip and face of the hammer. Zoe inhaled sharply at the sight, then noticed something else. She tapped the photo, pinching it between her thumb and index finger to zoom in.

In the claw at the rear of the hammer was matted, chestnut-coloured hair.

He's going to find out who's naughty or nice, she thought. *Merry fucking Christmas, everyone.*

She knew what it meant. He hadn't been much more subtle when they met to discuss the job. At the time, Zoe thought she could breeze in, make demands and breeze back out. And it had worked. To a point.

The breezing in had worked. The conversation with the client went well. Then it came time to discuss the finances of the job. For a moment, Zoe had thought she might take a leaf out of Violet's book and asked for more money. He'd agreed but the agreement came with a threat. Fail and you won't see January.

Apparently this text was a quick note to confirm the method of her execution should she fail.

But she wouldn't fail. Couldn't fail.

She shook her head, trying to shake the whole train of thought as she closed the image.

Breakfast arrived as Zoe distracted herself by sifting through a few messages from friends and checking on the data logs from last night. There were discrepancies, she thought, as she chewed her toast.

Agatha had left Korkus' room fifteen minutes after Zoe had landed in the snowdrift. Her sister had obviously upgraded her privileges since she'd gone through a staff entrance and through to the garage. Smug bitch probably thought she'd covered her tracks, but Zoe was better this time.

Then she'd gone back to the third floor only to leave again ten minutes later. Then back to her room, where she'd been ever since.

Gran had been in the room with Zoe until after one a.m. She felt bad at seeing this. Bad that they had regressed to her being nursed like a toddler, but mostly bad at her utter inability to adult successfully.

Well, she had to do something. There was no way she would let some *Point Break* wannabe cave her head in over an obsolete technology. She was Zoe fucking Zimmerman. She could do this. In her pyjamas and in bed if necessary.

She poured another coffee and switched on the hotel CCTV. In the breakfast room, Zoe could see her Gran, plate piled high with bacon and sausages.

'Getting her money's worth' she liked to call it. Zoe

grinned at the thought but stopped in her tracks when a picture arrived from her sister.

It was a cassette. Gift wrapped, in a manner of speaking, with a bow.

The message underneath read:

I got this to keep you out of trouble. Once I know what's on it I'll dispose of it. It's for your own good.

Zoe was in the hallway screaming at Agatha's closed door in under ten seconds. By the time her sister opened the door, Zoe was no longer using sentences, the words all running together in a torrent of helpless fury.

Agatha said nothing in her defence. She said nothing to calm the situation. She just waited for Zoe to stop screaming, kissed her fingertips and touched Zoe's cheek before closing the door in her face.

Zoe screamed.

People in the surrounding suites peaked out their doors, scared and intrigued by the commotion. Zoe ignored them and flounced back into her suite, slamming the door behind her.

And then, with the adrenaline washing around her system and the fury at her sister at its peak, Zoe had what alcoholics refer to as 'a moment of clarity'.

She took out her phone as she walked, bringing up the security feed for reception. There was Gran on her way back from breakfast. Perfect. She had a plan. And it started with a text message.

FOURTEEN

THE HOTEL MANAGER stood in the corner of the restaurant. Everything was going like clockwork. The ball last night had been a resounding success, breakfast was wrapping up, and every sign pointed to Christmas dinner going swimmingly.

There were no waiters with hangovers, no bellboys with the flu. It might be the first time in as long as he could remember his ulcer wasn't giving him grief.

His phone vibrated in his pocket. As he read the message, his face betrayed nothing of its contents. But as he moved away from the restaurant, he took a packet of antacids from his waistcoat pocket and put three in his mouth.

ZOE PROPPED another pillow behind her head and opened her laptop, the hotel systems dropping like flies as she plugged in to every aspect of the place. She quickly changed the access logs to show that she had left her room and gone to the spa, while keeping an eye on her Gran in reception in a second window.

THE RECEPTIONIST WAS TRYING to look busy while simultaneously using her computer to wish her friends Happy Christmas on Facebook. The breakfasters had all but left, and there was no real expectation that the receptionist would do anything like work for another twenty minutes or so.

Until the emergency pager on the desk buzzed.

Room 160. Burst pipe.

Shit.

The receptionist craned left and right to find someone to attend, but when no-one appeared she jogged off to deal with it herself.

ZOE NURSED a hot chocolate as she watched the receptionist vacate her post. She continued watching as Gran stood up, slipped behind the desk and into the back room.

For a moment, Zoe hesitated. This was her grandmother. Was she really going to go through with this part of the plan?

She had to.

Her finger came down on the 'return' key and the script she'd been writing executed itself. The hotel's log now contained two additional entries, both from different rooms and both relating to items of value going missing. One entry made specific note of a suspicious person matching Gran's description seen loitering in the vicinity.

She flicked to the CCTV and watched the manager making his way down the labyrinthine corridors to reception. Nodding, she accessed her Gran's records held by the hotel and changed her emergency contact phone number so it was one digit short.

Changing the view, Zoe saw the receptionist walking back from her pointless trip to room 160. Zoe buzzed the receptionist's pager once more, telling her there was a rush on reception, and saw her pace change from a dawdle to a jog.

AGATHA HAD dead bolted the door to prevent Zoe getting in after their little altercation in the corridor. She'd left the cassette in a drawer in the kitchen and gone in the shower, having fitted so much additional security that, should an errant mouse attempt an incursion, she'd have him grabbed by the ear and up in front of the mouse council faster than he could say 'cheese'.

She regretted having to do this to her sister, but as she'd said to her so many times before, it was for her own good. She hated having to be the grown up, but apparently she was stuck with it.

Her phone vibrated, and she ignored it for a second,

putting her hair up in a towel and slipping into t-shirt and tracksuit bottoms. It would be Zoe and it would enhance her little sister's irritation if Agatha took a moment.

Slippers on and moment taken, Agatha picked up her phone and answered it.

Two and a half seconds after that, she sprinted out of the room and went hurtling towards the stairs.

Zoe couldn't bring herself to smile at Agatha's panic. She knew that, if the roles were reversed and she was the one receiving the phone call that Gran was being detained until the police arrived, she would have reacted in exactly the same way.

She pulled on her slippers as she tapped away at her laptop, systematically dismantling every single one of her sisters security measures. Zoe stopped short of leaving a Trojan on Agatha's computer. There were some things even she would consider beyond the pale.

Once she was happy everything was as it should be, Zoe confirmed everyone's locations. Gran was in the security office with the manager, receptionist and head of security. Agatha was exiting the stairs at the far side of reception.

Perfect.

Zoe took Agatha's present from her suitcase and the access-all-areas keycard from the dining table and walked straight out of her room and into Agatha's. It was almost identical to her own suite but everything was on the opposite side and, thankfully, Agatha had brought precious little to clutter the place up.

Within three minutes, Zoe had located the cassette, pocketed it and replaced it with Agatha's Christmas present.

Moments later she was out of the suite and back in her own.

Checking her laptop, she could see Agatha in the room with Gran. She looked absolutely furious. Hands waving, the towel holding her wet hair drooping to one side. Even without the aid of an audio feed, Zoe knew the phrases 'you have no idea who you're dealing with' and 'we work with some of the best lawyers in the world' would be tripping from her lips right about now.

THE MANAGER practically ran from the security office back to his own. This wasn't how it was supposed to be. Weird old ladies wandering behind reception weren't that unusual, but complaints, evidence, witnesses… he didn't need any of this on Christmas morning.

He clicked 'print' and the evidence rolled off the printer. He emptied four more antacid tablets into his mouth and steeled himself for round two.

As SOON AS the manager walked back into the security office, Zoe did two things. Firstly, she deleted all traces of the complaints from the system and secondly, she let the maid into her room to tidy up and clear away the breakfast things.

In the meantime, she placed the cassette on what appeared to be a tiny reel-to-reel, which she plugged in to her computer. A few clicks later, and it was spinning quickly and causing the computer to emit a noise that was a little like someone removing R2-D2's testicles with a hacksaw.

The maid ignored it as she buzzed around and, having finished transferring the data, Zoe took the cassette to the writing desk in the corner, opened one of the drawers, and took out a gorgeously thick envelope. On it she wrote her own address and then placed the cassette inside and licked it closed.

As the maid was about to leave, Zoe stopped her.

"I don't suppose you could post this for me?" she asked.

"Of course, miss," said the maid.

"It'll need to be in a more padded envelope," she continued. Zoe grabbed three twenty pound notes and counted them into the maid's hand. "It's very important that happens."

"I understand, miss," said the maid, pausing so as not to appear too eager to snatch such a welcome tip. "I'll make sure it's in a padded envelope. Next day delivery might not happen, though. It being Christmas."

Zoe smiled. "I understand. But you'll make sure it gets there as quickly as possible."

"If I have to deliver it by hand, miss," said the maid.

Zoe laughed. "There's another hundred in it for you if you do," she said.

The maid looked at her as if she couldn't decide which fork in the road to take, then nodded and took the money and the envelope.

Even if the damned thing got lost in the post, Zoe could recreate it from the copy she'd made. But it was Christmas and it was nice to be nice.

A moment later the phone in the lounge began to ring.

"Excuse me, I've got to take this," she said with a smile.

The maid nodded and let herself out.

AGATHA SCREAMED INCOHERENTLY, which exacerbated the head of security's hangover something chronic. Gran looked like Miss Marple on Tramadol and when asked any direct question would just say 'I thought it was the gift shop, dear'.

The hysteria had reached fever pitch and finally the manager had snapped and shouted for everyone to stop.

Agatha stared daggers at him. Gran seemed genuinely to have been spiked with something that was, at the very least, reserved for equine veterinary medicine.

"This woman," he said, stabbing his index finger in Gran's direction, "was caught by my security *this far*," he held his thumb and forefinger a few centimetres apart, "from the hotel safe."

Agatha held up her hand and shook her head, loosening the towel still further.

"And a woman fitting her description has been linked to items going missing from two other rooms," he added, before sitting back triumphantly in his seat.

"You are lacking three things," said Agatha, removing the towel from her head and beginning to fold it. "Firstly, you are lacking a crime. Being in the same room as a safe does not constitute breaking into a safe. Was the safe broken into?"

"Well... no... but..."

Agatha slammed her palm on the table. "No. And secondly, you don't have any evidence whatsoever. What was taken from the other rooms?"

"I can check," he said quickly.

"Check away," she said, turning to Gran before continuing. "Check her room if you like." She stared frantically at the old woman, looking for confirmation.

Gran gave the slightest nod of her head.

"Check all of her bags." Agatha was relaxing into her monologue, feeling like a proper lawyer delivering her closing argument. "Tear the suite apart and you will not find a damned thing that doesn't belong to her."

"Well..." the manager was deflating by the second.

"Finally, you are lacking the I.Q. to win a battle of wits with a cucumber. I pray whichever house-Gods the staff who work here hold dear intervene on this mortal coil so you find yourself sacked on Christmas Day and only manage to find work running a Travel Lodge whose sole clientele is made up of men from stag parties. If by some quirk of fate this doesn't happen then I promise you this... I promise that I will make it my life's mission to ensure you never rise further than a rat on a fatberg."

The manager looked like he had just been punched in the brain. He sat for a long moment in silence, his eyes flicking here and there as if he was trying to come up with an answer, something... anything that would stop this horrid woman from speaking. In the end he gave up and just went on the attack.

"RIGHT!" he shouted. "I'm calling the police. I am not paid enough to deal with situations like this," he lied. "If I was, I'd give you the benefit of the doubt. But the complainants, as you can see, are fairly adamant."

He placed the documents he had printed on the desk in front of them and Agatha snatched them as he dialled 999.

"Which service do you require?" asked Zoe with a bad Brummie accent in the manager's ear.

"Police," he replied.

"Hold, please," was the response.

"What's the location of your emergency?" asked a much younger woman with a less distinct accent but one that was significantly closer to Zoe's own.

The manager told her and then explained the nature of the emergency.

"Sir, you really consider this to be an emergency?" asked Zoe down the line.

"Well, yes," he said. His eyes flicked to Agatha, who was doing something on her phone. Her fingers were moving faster than he'd ever seen on anyone over the age of thirteen. "It's very important," he added.

"Important." A note of irritation crept into Zoe's voice. "But not an emergency. Do you know what the last call I took was? A man had stabbed his wife through the shoulder with a carving knife. THAT is an emergency. This is… is… bullshit," said Zoe. "Looking at our maps, you're snowed in up there anyway, so it will not happen. Deal with it yourself and be glad I'm not going to prosecute you for wasting police time."

With that, she hung up.

"Yes," said the manager to the dead receiver. "Yes… Okay… No, I understand… Yes… We can hold her here if necessary… No, we could just let her stay in her room if you prefer… Okay… Great… See you then."

He made a show of pretending to hang up.

"Two things," said Agatha. "One…" she pointed to the complaint. "There is no room 195. These people don't exist."

The obvious truth of this drained the colour from the head of security's face.

"Two," Agatha continued. "I've checked your record on the hotel server and there is no complaint. And I don't mean I've deleted it. I mean it never existed. You can't create a complaint for a room that doesn't exist. System doesn't allow it."

The manager nodded silently. He knew all of that was true. What the fuck was happening?

FIFTEEN

"DID YOU?" Agatha asked, almost silently. "Did you actually nick that stuff?"

"My memory's not what it was," Gran replied.

Agatha seethed quietly as the two of them waited for the lift.

"Hi. you two!" Zoe said brightly, shuffling across to them in hotel slippers, robe and towel-wrapped hair. "Merry Christmas!"

Agatha had left her towel in the security office and was cultivating anger-curls like a brunette medusa.

Zoe went in for a hug, with Gran reciprocating, and Agatha standing tree-like and motionless.

"Did you have a good night's sleep, darling?" asked Gran.

Zoe nodded and gave Gran a kiss on the cheek.

"Been to the spa," said Zoe pointedly. "You should check it out."

The three of them confirmed their Christmas dinner

arrangements and parted ways once more, with Gran heading off one way and Zoe and Agatha the other.

"You know the spa's closed today?" asked Agatha, once they were out of earshot.

"Ah," said Zoe.

They walked in silence the rest of the way to the suites, but before Zoe turned to open her room, Agatha stopped her.

"Come in a minute, will you?" she asked.

Zoe glanced back at the safety of her own suite then, nodded and followed Agatha.

The two of them walked into the suite. Once inside, Zoe ditched the robe and towel to reveal that she was fully dressed underneath, hair as dry as a bone. Agatha made a beeline for the kitchen and the drawer that had contained the cassette.

She placed the gift from Zoe on the dining table, then pulled out a chair and sat on it. She motioned for Zoe to sit opposite.

"That was smooth," said Agatha. "I mean… using Gran but not using Gran. Did you plan that from the start or just do it on the fly?"

Zoe shrugged, not sure what she wanted to reveal and what she didn't.

"Cards on the table?" asked Zoe.

"Please," said Agatha. "No more games."

"Same goes for you."

It was Agatha's turn to pause. Eventually she nodded.

"I fell off the third floor and nearly got an eyeful of your new boyfriend getting to fourth base," grinned Zoe.

"I don't understand basketball metaphors," said a po-faced Agatha.

"Neither do I."

Agatha cracked, smiling at last. "He didn't... handle the goods," she said. "I drugged him and switched the cassette for Queen's Greatest Hits from Gran's car."

Zoe burst out laughing. "I'd love to be there when the buyer tries to decode it."

"You dodged the question," said Agatha, still smiling.

"I did," said Zoe. "I planned what happened. In ten minutes. And the rest I did on the fly."

"And the police?"

"Yeah, that was me."

"And framing Gran?"

Zoe stuck up her two thumbs then pointed them to herself.

"She was always safe," said Zoe. "I had full control of the place and everyone in it."

"This from the woman who fell from the third floor last night?"

Zoe shrugged again.

"It was more dangerous than you thought," said Agatha. Her tone had changed. She was worried, Zoe thought, as she waited for her to go on.

"I have to tell you something." Agatha was clearly struggling with what she was about to say. "It *was* a risk because Gran..."

"Is a massive klepto?" asked Zoe.

"What?" Agatha gawped.

"I thought you didn't know," said Zoe.

"I thought *you* didn't know," said Agatha. "I always protected you—"

"Not always," said Zoe. "I mean, sometimes she was just forgetful and nicked stuff when we were there. But it was the weeks or months where she was missing for no reason that were the real giveaway."

Agatha sighed. She held Zoe's gaze, then a smile spread across her face and they both laughed.

"So we both knew. All this time," said Agatha.

"And I took all that into account when I executed the plan," said Zoe. "Or at least the last part of it…"

"Is that what your crew say? Execute the plan?" Agatha caught the note of criticism in her voice and backtracked. "I mean… It was professional. Slick even. No-one can beat me."

"I can." Zoe pointed to the gift on the table.

"Sometimes," Agatha corrected.

"You cheated," said Zoe. "I didn't know you were playing the game." She tipped the dining chair back, rocking on the back two legs.

"It's not a fucking game, sis," said Agatha.

"No, it's not. Sometimes you have to be a grown up." Zoe didn't look her sister in the eye as she spoke. She said the words carefully, as if they might scald her lips. "This job. I made a mistake when I took it. I guess you thought you were helping. Trying to protect me—"

"I researched him," interrupted Agatha. "The man you're doing the job for. I was terrified for you. I committed a crime for you."

Zoe nodded, still not looking at her. "And he would have killed you for it and then me for failing."

Agatha didn't speak.

"I… we… have a reputation. Of sorts. And delivering the tape means I get paid and neither of us has a problem. I had to take it from you. I did it…" She finally looked her sister in the eyes. "There are good people and there are bad people. And just because I sometimes break the law doesn't mean I'm a bad person."

"But you're a criminal," said Agatha. "If you break the law you're a criminal. It's as simple as that."

"No. It's not," said Zoe. "Don't get me wrong, I understand I'm not taking from the rich and giving to the poor. But the people who I steal from are…"

"Korkus is a monster," said Agatha. "And your client is worse, if anything."

"These are bad people," said Zoe. She stared at her fingernails, lost in thought. "But I'm not. And I get it. I understand why you do what you do to try and protect me. I love you and I stole the cassette back to protect you. And Gran."

Agatha looked like she might burst into tears.

"But mostly," a grave look passed onto Zoe's face. "Mostly… I did it because I'm better than you and I was showboating." She grinned and winked. "Just kidding!"

Agatha laughed nervously. "I could deliver it to him," she said eventually. "Instead of you…"

"This is my life. When it comes to pretending to be a stuntwoman I am a proponent of the epic fail but when it comes to being a whizkid…"

"Promise me something," said Agatha. "Promise me

that you'll avoid people like him. Promise me… promise me…"

"What?"

"Promise me you'll be careful, at least."

"I promise the last one," said Zoe.

Agatha nodded.

Zoe shoved the present over the table. "Open it."

Agatha opened the present. The tears that had been lurking behind her eyes finally made an appearance, overflowing and trickling down her cheeks.

It was a first generation iPod. Still sealed.

"Maybe we can get a headphone splitter for it?" asked Agatha.

SIXTEEN

QUINN KORKUS DIDN'T JOIN them for Christmas dinner. He tried, but decided to dine alone after Gran told him in no uncertain terms to 'fuck off'.

Fortunately for the Zimmerman sisters he seemed blissfully unaware that anything untoward had happened to any of his possessions.

The manager, for the sake of his ulcers, comped their entire stay. Over the course of Christmas dinner Agatha put pressure on Zoe to spend the money for the three of them to go on a mini-break together, which, after the Christmas pudding, she agreed to.

When the coffees had been and gone, Agatha excused herself to go and pack and Zoe sat with Gran at the table, looking out at the snowscape that surrounded them.

"Did you have a good time, Gran?"

"I just like spending time with you two, sweetie," said Gran.

Zoe made a noise like a buzzer going off. "Wrong

answer, septuagenarian. Guess again but be careful…" she adopted a faux-American-game-show-host-accent. "One wrong answer might see you put in an old people's home!"

"Come here, buggerlugs." Gran made a grab for her but Zoe ducked, laughing.

Gran stared at her. "I did. I really did. You know what I liked most?"

Zoe shook her head and took a sip of wine.

"I think you two might finally have grown up."

Zoe squinted at her. "What do you mean?" she asked.

"It suits me sometimes to play my age, if you know what I mean?"

"I think I do."

"I know you both know… or have your suspicions about… certain aspects of my past."

Zoe's eyes widened. "Have you told—"

"Whether I have or haven't told your sister has no bearing on this conversation," Gran shut her down. "This is between you and me. And what's between Agatha and me is… you know… anyway… I wasn't as talented as either of you. I've always encouraged you. Never judged you. Agatha had that sensibility. She knew the rules. Her world is built on them. You always knew the rules too. You just didn't give a shit about them."

Zoe laughed. No-one knew you like your family knew you. "It's a fair cop," she said.

"When I got here I noticed how relaxed they were to certain aspects of security," said Gran, with a twinkle in her eye. "The barman didn't even notice when I lifted that young man's wallet."

"I did," replied Zoe.

"Yes, you always were a little too observant. Nice counter-lift by the way."

"I've been practising," said Zoe, her cheeks reddening with the compliment.

"I was going to take the contents of the safe and then you two started acting up," said Gran. She sipped at her wine. "I noticed Agatha first, of course. That girl couldn't be a successful criminal if her life depended on it."

"Oh I don't know… I didn't notice until—"

"I know you didn't notice," Gran interrupted. "That's why you wound up sifting through my unmentionables in the bottom of my wardrobe."

Zoe had a flashback to the nipple tassels and remained silent.

"I couldn't be sure you two wouldn't wind up getting arrested so I had to put my little plan on ice," said Gran. "I wanted to make sure Agatha didn't get a little too self-righteous and actually have you arrested… for your own good… which is definitely something only *normal* people would say."

"That might have happened?" asked Zoe, eyes wide.

"She's very forthright," said Gran. "Anyway… I thought I better keep an eye on you and it was just as well I did after that crap you pulled on the balcony."

Zoe directed all her attention to the stem of her wine glass.

"I was watching you from the conservatory when

you fell. I nearly needed a second hip replacement the speed I had to get out there and cover you up. If anyone had seen you in that maid's outfit…"

"Thanks, Gran," said Zoe. "I mean it."

Gran shook her head. "No need to thank me, but do you know how long I had to hang around reception to give you the idea to frame me."

"Wait, what?" asked Zoe. "You're saying you were playing mind games with me?"

"Manipulating you, darling," Gran grinned. "Been doing it my whole life. It's part of being a parent."

"Genius," said Zoe, clapping her hands.

"And the whole 'little old lady lost' act," said Gran, "was just to sell it for as long as you needed."

"Did you know Agatha had…" Zoe paused, looking over her shoulder. "…what I was looking for?"

"No," Gran admitted. "But I knew you needed her off your back to get it."

Zoe raised her glass and Gran clinked it with her own.

"Sometimes you have to nudge your kids in the right direction. I think Agatha will be twice the woman I've been," said Gran. "And I think you'll be a thousand times the thief I was. But know your limits. Know your friends. Don't trust easily, but once trust is earned pay it back."

"I feel like I should be writing this down."

"If you did write it down it'd be on that damned phone," said Gran.

"Well, yes," said Zoe, reaching into her pocket. "You should let me show you…"

"Darling, I don't need a phone to stay two steps ahead of you or your sister."

"Wait… what?" Zoe nearly spilled her wine.

"Don't underestimate what you think is beneath you. Sometimes the old ways work better."

"Buh…" was all Zoe managed.

"If they didn't you might have frozen to death."

"This is a *lot* to unpack," said Zoe.

Gran shrugged.

"If you tell your sister any of it I'll just pretend to be old," she said.

Zoe charged her glass. "It's the perfect disguise," she said. "To being old."

Gran rolled her eyes and clinked her cup of tea. "So where are we going on holiday then?"

ACKNOWLEDGMENTS

I'm always surprised and humbled by the help, insight and support that all of my friends and loved ones have shown me when it comes to my writing and this little tome is no exception.

James Whitman for his next-level insight as an editor. Thank you not just for making my writing better but for coining the term 'Maxwellism' - and not as an insult.

Michael Brett for being on the receiving end of the roughest of drafts, always offering encouragement and never saying 'sounds shit to me'.

Sam Hartburn, Matt Austin, Elaine Jinks-Turner and Brenda West, for all the time you give without complaining in the pursuit of proofreading. Your contributions are absolutely invaluable.

The Kilchester Irregulars - Claire Knight, Gordon McGhie, Sarah Jones, Dave Graham, Colman Keane, Meggy Roussell, Martin Greatbatch, Krissy Lee and Kristy Linderholm. Thank you for your encouragement and willingness to let me waffle at you. It can't be overstated how wonderful it feels that there are people out there that give as much of a shit about these characters as me.

Laura Swaddle for her graphic design insight, help and, above all, patience in the face of sometimes quite insane requests.

And of course Noddy Holder and Slade for being the best band to ever come out of the black country and without whom the Christmas would lose at least thirty three and a third per cent of its magic.

- A.M.

BIGGER
ACKNOWLEDGEMENTS

It is customary to ensure that the largest acknowledgement goes to my wife Eve. You are my favourite and my best. Christmas wouldn't be Christmas without you.

And Bruce Willis, obviously, because... Die Hard.

Printed in Great Britain
by Amazon